Acting Edition

The Visitor

Music by Tom Kitt

Lyrics by Brian Yorkey

Book by Kwame Kwei-Armah
and Brian Yorkey

FOR PRODUCTION INQUIRIES

UNITED STATES AND CANADA
info@concordtheatricals.com
1-866-979-0447

UNITED KINGDOM AND EUROPE
licensing@concordtheatricals.co.uk
020-7054-7298

Each title is subject to availability from Concord Theatricals Corp., depending upon country of performance. Please be aware that *THE VISITOR* may not be licensed by Concord Theatricals Corp. in your territory. Professional and amateur producers should contact the nearest Concord Theatricals Corp. office or licensing partner to verify availability.

THE VISITOR was originally developed by The Public Theater (Oskar Eustis, Artistic Director; Patrick Willingham, Executive Director) and received its world premiere production there, opening on October 14, 2021. The production was directed by Daniel Sullivan, with orchestrations by Jamshied Sharifi, scenic design by David Zinn, costume design by Toni-Leslie James, lighting design by Japhy Weideman, co-sound design by Jessica Paz & Sun Hee Kil, and co-video design by David Bengali & Hana S. Kim. The production stage manager was James Latus. The cast was as follows:

WALTER . . . . David Hyde Pierce

TAREK . . . . Ahmad Maksoud

ZAINAB . . . . Alysha Deslorieux

MOUNA . . . . Jacqueline Antaramian

ENSEMBLE . . . . Robert Ariza, Anthony Chan, Delius Doherty, C.K. Edwards, Will Erat, Brandon Espinoza, Sean Ewing, Marla Louissaint, Dimitri Joseph Moïse, Takafumi Nikaido, Paul Pontrelli, Katie Terza

THE VISITOR is based on the Groundswell Productions and Participant Media motion picture written by Thomas McCarthy.

CHARACTERS

PRINCIPAL

WALTER – White, middle-aged, stoic
TAREK – Arabic, mid twenties, filled with the joy of life and music
ZAINAB – Senegalese, mid twenties, does not trust easily
MOUNA – mid forties, Tarek's mother, a gentle soul

ENSEMBLE

A minimum of 12 actors are required for the ensemble: 2 women, 10 men.

CHARLES
STUDENTS
LECTURERS
NEW YORKERS
SINGER
COLLEAGUE
SPEAKER
ATTENDEES
DRUM CIRCLE
POLICE OFFICERS
MUSICIANS
TRANSIT COPS
ECONOMISTS
CONFERENCE CHAIR
DETAINEES
NASIM
GUARDS
VENDORS
ZINZI
CUSTOMERS

MUSICAL NUMBERS

ACT ONE

ACT TWO

ACT ONE

[MUSIC NO. 00 – PROLOGUE]

(A drumroll. Then another. Then a third one which becomes a steady beat...)

*(Voices grow as **STUDENTS** and **LECTURERS** begin to appear.)*

ENSEMBLE GROUP 2.

HERE I AM

ENSEMBLE GROUP 1.

HERE I AM

ENSEMBLE GROUP 2.

HERE I AM

ENSEMBLE GROUP 1.

HERE I AM

ENSEMBLE GROUP 2.

HERE I AM...

ENSEMBLE GROUP 1.

HERE I AM...

ENSEMBLE GROUP 1 & 2.

HERE I AM!

*(**STUDENTS** sit and turn to look at **WALTER** who is concluding a lecture at Connecticut College where he teaches. He is lost, mid-lecture. The sudden silence returns him to reality.)*

WALTER. So the post-World War Two academic movement referred to as neoclassical synthesis, absorbing the macroeconomic thought of John Maynard Keynes, resulted in the theories and models termed...

[MUSIC NO. 01 – WAKE UP]

(Without pause, he sings.)

WAKE UP – YOU IN THE BACK ROW –
YOU'RE DROOLING DOWN YOUR CHIN.

...Neo-Keynesian economics. That theory was developed by John Hicks and Maurice Allais and popularized by the mathematical economist Paul Samuelson. The process...

WAKE UP – YOU, WITH THE HAIR, THERE –
SOMEONE POKE HER WITH A PIN.

...began soon after the publication of Keynes' General Theory with the IS/LM model-investment.

WAKE UP, YOU LITTLE SNOT RAGS –
PRETEND YOU HAVE A CLUE.
IF I HAVE TO LISTEN TO THIS PAP,
THIS DULL AND DREARY CRAP,
THEN SO DO YOU.

AND IT'S NOT LIKE I CAN BLAME THEM
IF THEY LEAVE THE ROOM –
THE MIND DEPARTS,
JUST UP AND DRIFTS AWAY
IT'S NATURAL TO FLEE
FROM THIS OPPRESSIVE GLOOM
THIS BOGUS INTELLECTUAL DISPLAY
THE ONLY THING THAT CHANGES
IS THE DAY.

*(Lights. **WALTER** searches.)*

I'm sorry, where was I? Hicks, of course. John Hicks continued with adaptations of the supply and demand model –

WAKE UP, YOU SLEEPY SHITHEADS –
THIS WORLD IS SPINNING FAST.
YOU MAY THINK YOU HAVE IT SUSSED
THAT LIFE IS GOOD AND JUST,
BUT IT WON'T LAST.
BLINK TWICE IN ALL YOUR LAUGHTER
AND YOUR HAPPY-EVER-AFTER
FLIES RIGHT PAST.

GOD, TRY TO FOCUS, WALTER, ON THE POINTS AT HAND
THIS COURSE THAT YOU HAVE TAUGHT FOR TWENTY
    YEARS.
DON'T THINK ABOUT THE DAY YOU BOUGHT HER
    WEDDING BAND,
OR THE TRIP THAT YOU TWO MADE ONCE TO ALGIERS,
OR THE WAY THE TIME BETWEEN JUST DISAPPEARS...

A specific example of this is the consumer theory of individual demand. That's it. See you next week.

(A **STUDENT** *approaches him tentatively and holds out a paper. The* **STUDENT** *is wearing a kufi – a brimless cap worn by men in many Muslim communities. He gives the paper to* **WALTER**.*)*

They were due two weeks ago.

STUDENT. But...

WALTER. I'm sorry, I can't accept it now.

STUDENT. I...

WALTER. I'm sorry.

(As the **STUDENT** *turns to go.)* You know – there are resources, on campus. For foreign students. Who need extra help.

STUDENT. I was born in Trenton.

WALTER. Oh. I'm sorry.

STUDENT. You're sorry I was born in Trenton? Yeah, me too. You know, it's almost April and you still haven't given us the syllabus.

WALTER. I know.

(The **STUDENT** *goes.)*

WAKE UP – YOU WITH THE LECTURE –
THE DAY'S NOT OVER YET –
NO TIME FOR REMEMBRANCE OR REGRET.

[MUSIC NO. 01A – INTO WALTER'S OFFICE]

ENSEMBLE GROUP 2. *(Offstage.)*
HERE I AM...

ENSEMBLE GROUP 1. *(Offstage.)*
HERE I AM...

(A knock at the door.)

CHARLES. There you are, Walter, you got a minute?

WALTER. Sure.

CHARLES. Shelley can't make it down to the NYU conference to present your paper. I'm going to need you to cover for her – she's been put on bed rest until she has the baby.

WALTER. I wish I could –

CHARLES. Come on, Walter. You only have to be there for the week.

WALTER. Now is not a very good time, Charles.

CHARLES. You co-authored the paper and the dean wants it presented. He wants to keep Shelley on track for tenure.

WALTER. I just don't think I can, with finals, and my book...

CHARLES. The dean wants you to present it. You are only teaching one class.

WALTER. So I can stay focused on my book.

CHARLES. Well – if the research is getting in the way – maybe you should think of a sabbatical –

WALTER. I don't believe in sabbaticals. You know that.

CHARLES. I know. I tried to get you to take one after Sarah.

WALTER. I know.

CHARLES. Maybe now that it's been a couple years…

WALTER. Don't!

CHARLES. …being back in New York again might…

WALTER. Charles, the truth is this is really Shelley's paper. I just agreed to put my name on it because she asked me to. I'm not remotely prepared to present it.

CHARLES. It's microfinance, it's how you made your name. Look. Walter. You can take it up with the dean if you want, but as your friend, I wouldn't advise it.

WALTER. Fine.

CHARLES. Great.

> (**CHARLES** *goes.*)

> **[MUSIC NO. 01B – SUBWAY TRANSITION #1]**

> (*Transition to:*)

> (*New York Penn Station.*)

> (**WALTER** *gets off the subway. A* **BUCKET DRUMMER** *is doing his thing. Some* **NEW YORKERS** *stop to watch.* **WALTER** *notices the* **DRUMMER** *fleetingly but keeps it moving without pause.*)

ENSEMBLE. *(Offstage.)*
HERE I AM...
HERE I AM

(Lights.)

(Walter's apartment.)

*(Keys still in hand, **WALTER** enters his apartment. He notices immediately that the lights are on.)*

*(Before he can take a step to investigate, **ZAINAB**, in a dressing gown, enters the room.)*

*(**ZAINAB** screams. **WALTER** shouts.)*

ZAINAB. *(Covering herself hurriedly.)* Stay away from me!

*(**WALTER** turns away.)*

*(Overlapping **WALTER**.)* Stay away!

WALTER. *(Overlapping.)* It's okay. It's okay. I'm not –

ZAINAB. My boyfriend is coming home!

WALTER. I'm not going to hurt you.

ZAINAB. Who are you? How did you get in?

WALTER. My name is Walter Vale. I have keys. It's my –

*(**TAREK** has entered, unseen to **WALTER**, and grabs him.)*

TAREK. What the fuck? Are you okay?

ZAINAB. I'm fine. He was just –

TAREK. *(Shaking **WALTER**.)* Did you touch her? Did you touch her?

WALTER. No! No!

ZAINAB. He didn't touch me! But he has keys.

WALTER. It's my apartment.

TAREK. What do you mean, it's yours?

WALTER. *(Holds up his keys.)* I've owned it for twenty-five years. I live in Connecticut. I haven't been down here in a very long time.

TAREK. Are you Ivan's friend?

WALTER. Ivan? Who is Ivan?

TAREK. He rented us this place. He said it belonged to his friend who was out of town.

WALTER. I don't know who Ivan is, but this is my apartment. I assure you.

> *(**TAREK** pauses. Fear hits. He looks to **ZAINAB**. He readjusts.)*

TAREK. Oh! Alright look, there must have been a mix up, we'll get out right away.

WALTER. Alright.

ZAINAB. I told you –

TAREK. We don't want to cause any trouble.

WALTER. Okay. I'll...let you gather your things.

TAREK. Right.

WALTER. Okay.

[MUSIC NO. 02 – TAREK AND ZAINAB]

> *(**TAREK** hurries into the bedroom, and **ZAINAB** follows.)*

> *(Split stage:)*

> *(**WALTER** stays in the main room.)*

ZAINAB. I knew this would happen!

(They pack furiously as they continue the argument.)

*(In the main room, **WALTER** looks around, finds a throw on the couch, folds it –)*

ZAINAB.

JE VOUS L'AI DIT

TAREK. I know you have.

ZAINAB.

JE VOUS L'AI DIT TOUJOURS...

TAREK. I know, I know.

ZAINAB.

YOU NEVER LISTEN TO ME.

TAREK. *(Spoken, in rhythm.)*

I DO, I SWEAR, I DO.

ZAINAB.

QU'EST-CE QU'ON PEUT FAIRE?
QU'EST-CE QU'ON PEUT FAIRE?

TAREK.

WE KNEW THIS PLACE WOULD NOT BE FOREVER
WE HAVEN'T FOUND THAT YET
WE SAID WE'D STAY 'TIL WE HAD TO GO –
DON'T FORGET

> *(**WALTER** notices some of their items. He gathers them.)*

ZAINAB.

YOU ALWAYS MAKE THIS PROMISE
YOU ALWAYS SAY TO TRUST YOU
AND STILL, WE'RE ALWAYS ON THE RUN

THIS CITY IS HEARTLESS
THIS CITY IS COLD
THE SECOND WE LET OUR GUARD DOWN WE'RE DONE.

(**TAREK** *pauses in his packing.*)

(**WALTER** *pauses, staring at one CD in particular – the picture of a smiling woman at a piano on the cover.*)

TAREK.
SOMEDAY, SOME PLACE WILL BE OURS FOREVER –
LET'S JUST SURVIVE THIS NIGHT

WE'VE ALWAYS LANDED UP ON OUR FEET –

SO – ALL RIGHT?
ALL RIGHT?

ZAINAB. *(Finally.)* All right.

(*As they finish packing, lights rise on* **WALTER.**)

(*The piano refrain plays gently. Amid gathering Tarek and Zainab's stuff,* **WALTER** *notices a few of his wife's CDs on the table. He picks them up and looks at them almost unemotionally.*)

(**TAREK** *and* **ZAINAB** *drag all their worldly possessions into the next room, toward the door.* **TAREK** *hoists two djembes.*)

(**WALTER** *hurriedly sets the CDs aside.* **TAREK** *sees this.*)

TAREK. Sorry about the mess. You have so much great music here. You've got a lot of her.

(*Points to the CD in* **WALTER**'s *hand.*)

Who is she?

WALTER. Umm...

TAREK. She's amazing.

WALTER. Yes. She is... You're a musician.

TAREK. Yes. Are you?

WALTER. No.

TAREK. Oh – I thought, with all the piano music maybe –

WALTER. I am not a musician.

TAREK. Oh. Well. Again, Walter – our apologies.

[MUSIC NO. 03 – ZAINAB'S APOLOGY]

ZAINAB. We would be very grateful – if you would not call the police.

WALTER. Alright, but who is this Ivan?

TAREK. He's the guy that we –

ZAINAB. *(Cuts him off.)* You don't have to worry about him. He is no longer around.

WALTER. I do have to worry about him. Miss, he's renting my apartment to strangers.

ZAINAB.

    I APOLOGIZE, WALTER,
    FOR OUR TRESPASS IN YOUR FLAT
    FOR YOUR HURT, AND CONFUSION,
    OUR UNTHINKABLE INTRUSION,
    I APOLOGIZE FOR THAT.
    WE SHOULD HAVE MADE MORE COURTEOUS AMENDS,
    AS WE PACKED AWAY OUR LITTLE ODDS AND ENDS –
    THAT WASN'T RIGHT.
    SO I APOLOGIZE, WALTER –
    GOOD NIGHT.

WALTER. Do you know where you are going to go?

ZAINAB.

    WE'VE HAD SEVEN HOMES IN A YEAR...
    NUMBER EIGHT WILL SOON BE NEAR

WE'RE QUITE GOOD AT KNOWING HOW TO DISAPPEAR
WE BOTH KNOW HOW TO FLEE IN FEAR –

(Stops herself.)

I APOLOGIZE, I DO –
FOR WHAT WE'VE PUT YOU THROUGH –
GOOD NIGHT,
GOOD LUCK, TO YOU...

TAREK. Take care, Walter.

> *(****TAREK**** and ****ZAINAB**** leave the apartment. ****WALTER**** picks up the CD case again.)*

WALTER.
WE KNEW THIS PLACE WOULDN'T BE FOREVER –
A YOUTHFUL HOME FOR TWO –
IT SEEMS NO MORE THAN SOME EMPTY ROOMS WITHOUT
   YOU.

> *(Split stage:)*

> *(****TAREK**** and ****ZAINAB**** appear out on the street. ****ZAINAB**** is finishing a phone call.)*

TAREK. Wait, maybe you should call your Auntie Marieme.

ZAINAB. Auntie Marieme? *(Re: their relationship.)* She hates this. Think she'll let us shack up there?

> *(****WALTER**** moves to an open window – it is clear he can hear them. He's trying to catch their attention, but they cannot see him. ****WALTER**** has Zainab's sketchbook in his hand.)*

TAREK. Well, call your cousin, the fun one.

ZAINAB. The fun one is in jail.

TAREK. Again?

ZAINAB. Tarek.

> (**WALTER** *has left the window and now approaches the couple, just as they are moving off. He stops them.*)

WALTER. Hello.

TAREK. Oh. Hello.

WALTER. You left your sketchbook.

> (*He holds it out although unsure whose pad it is. Warily,* **ZAINAB** *takes it.*)

ZAINAB. Thank you.

WALTER. These are your designs?

ZAINAB. Yes, I make jewelry.

TAREK. Here look at this – isn't she talented?

> (*He shows his bracelet.*)

WALTER. It's quite beautiful.

ZAINAB. Thank you.

> (*They stare at him unsure what he is about to say.*)

WALTER. Do you have a place to stay?

TAREK. Yeah, yeah, we will…

ZAINAB. It won't be a problem.

WALTER. Stay at my apartment. For the night. Some time to sort the situation out. Look, it's late, it's cold out.

ZAINAB. No. Thank you.

TAREK. Habibti –

ZAINAB. (*Turns away from* **WALTER**.) Tarek, we don't know that we can trust this man.

TAREK. Trust him? We could be in jail already.

ZAINAB. This could be a set up. The police could be waiting.

TAREK. This is no setup. Look at him.

*(They turn to **WALTER**.)*

Thank you, Walter. We'll stay just for the night.

WALTER. Okay. I'll help you with your bags.

*(**WALTER** goes.)*

ZAINAB. Tarek…

TAREK. Habibti. What choice do we have? Besides, I think he likes us.

ZAINAB. You, perhaps.

TAREK. Everyone likes me.

ZAINAB. Yes. I know.

[MUSIC NO. 03A – SUBWAY TRANSITION #2 (ASHHAD)]

(They go.)

*(Lights change to the next morning, the street below Walter's apartment. From the subway, we hear the beautiful sounds of a **SINGER** chanting, accompanied by a **BUCKET DRUMMER**:)*

SINGER. *(In Arabic.)*

AMAN	آمن
AMAN	آمن
AMAN	آمن
AMAN	آمن
ASHHAD…	أشهد
ASHHAD…	أشهد
ASHHAD…	أشهد

(**WALTER** *enters the platform and stops to look at the* **SINGER** *and* **DRUMMER** *as they vibe beautifully together. He watches and listens intently.*)

(*An academic* **COLLEAGUE** *enters the platform and stops beside him, but* **WALTER** *doesn't notice him until he speaks.*)

COLLEAGUE. Walter, hey, heading to the conference?

WALTER. Yes.

COLLEAGUE. Are you presenting today?

WALTER. No, no, Thursday. It's Caroline Vance this morning, on microfinance in China.

COLLEAGUE. Of course. She's great. Walter, second car from the front puts you right at the exit. Boom, first out of the station.

WALTER. Okay, good to know.

(**WALTER** *lingers with the* **MUSICIANS**, *watching, then sings quietly.*)

HERE I AM...

ENSEMBLE.
HERE I AM...

WALTER.	**ENSEMBLE.**
HERE I AM...	AM...

(*Lights.*)

[MUSIC NO. 04 – IN THE MIDDLE OF THE MIDDLE ROW]

(*Hotel Ballroom.*)

(**WALTER** *is in his seat in the middle of the middle row, a three-ring binder in his* *lap, surrounded by other* **ATTENDEES** *as a* **SPEAKER** *presents at the lectern.)*

SPEAKER. In spite of the remarkable economic growth which China has experienced over the past three decades, more than one hundred and fifty-three million of its inhabitants still live on less than 1.25 U.S. dollars per day. That's less than your morning latte folks...

(The **SPEAKER** *fades into the music as* **WALTER**'s *attention drifts.)*

WALTER.
THAT ZAINAB TERRIFIES ME –
SHE'S BRILLIANT, YOUNG, AND FIERCE.
THOSE LOOKS SHE SHOOTS ME PIERCE ME TO THE QUICK,
AND I FEEL THICK,
AND I DEFER,
BUT HE LOVES HER.

(The **SPEAKER** *fades back in.)*

SPEAKER. When I checked with the oracle, Twitter, this morning, Chinese policy still restricts microfinance.

(...but fades away again as **WALTER**'s *attention shifts.)*

WALTER.
THAT TAREK HAS A SWEETNESS
HE FILLS A ROOM WITH LIGHT
MY GOD, TO BE THAT BRIGHT AND BE THAT FREE –
WAS THAT ONCE ME?
THE WAY WE WERE –
THE WAY HE LOVES HER...
HE LOVES HER.

AND HERE I AM,
HERE I AM,

WALTER.
IN A SUIT, IN A BALLROOM
OF A TASTEFUL, WELL-LIT, BROWN-AND-BEIGE HOTEL,
PRETENDING THAT I'M HERE TO LISTEN WELL,
KNOWING THAT NOBODY ELSE CAN HEAR
THIS RHYTHM IN MY EAR...

SPEAKER. These conservative regulations have a very serious effect on wealth creation.

WALTER.
IN MY EAR...

> (**WALTER** *begins to drum, out of rhythm, on the binder. It is as if he is recalling a dynamic rhythmic passage of a classical piece.*)

SPEAKER. Let us compare this to other countries with looser regulations.

> (**WALTER** *goes away again.*)

WALTER.
THE TWO OF THEM SEEM FEARLESS,
AND BURNING WITH THEIR YOUTH,
WITH PASSION AND WITH TRUTH AND WITH DESIRE.
THAT BRIGHTEST FIRE
MAY SOMEDAY DIM,
BUT HE LOVES HER,
AND SHE LOVES HIM.

BUT HERE I AM,
HERE I AM,
MAKING EV'RYTHING ROMANTIC,
WHILE TWO STRANGERS HAVE THE RUN OF MY SMALL FLAT
I GAVE THEM KEYS – AND WHY DID I DO THAT?
THEY'RE STEALING ALL I HAVE IN THERE, I BET –
OF COURSE, THEY HAVEN'T DONE THAT YET –

AND HERE I AM,
HERE I AM,
IN A SUIT, IN THIS CONFERENCE,
IN THE MIDDLE SEAT INSIDE THE MIDDLE ROW,
WITH NOWHERE MUCH OF NOTE THAT I CAN GO,
BUT WISHING I WERE ANYWHERE INSTEAD,
WITH THIS RHYTHM IN MY HEAD…

(He drums, a bit harder, and is shushed by a few **ATTENDEES.***)*

ATTENDEE.
SHHH!

WALTER.
IN MY HEAD…

THREE ATTENDEES.
SHH!

TWO ATTENDEES.
SHH!

WALTER.
HERE I AM…

ATTENDEE.
SHH!

TWO ATTENDEES.
SHH!

WALTER.
HERE I AM…

ENSEMBLE.
SHH! SHH! SHHH!

WALTER.
HERE I AM…

ENSEMBLE.
SHH! SHH! SHH!

*(**WALTER** resumes drumming, oblivious to the room...)*

SPEAKER & ENSEMBLE.
SHH!

*(Until they all, **SPEAKER** included, give him the biggest shush yet. Music stops, the drumming stops. A moment.)*

(Then, under his breath:)

WALTER. Assholes.

(Lights.)

[MUSIC NO. 04A – INTO WALTER'S APARTMENT]

*(The musical instruments gradually fade until all we are left with is a single drum – **TAREK**, practicing, in his underwear. **WALTER** enters, and **TAREK** finishes with a flourish.)*

TAREK. Hey Walter. I didn't know you would be home so soon. Sorry about the pants, I've been practicing like this since I was a kid.

WALTER. Really? Where was that?

TAREK. Michigan.

WALTER. Oh, you're from Michigan?

*(**TAREK** does not answer. **WALTER** can see that he won't, but he keeps gently digging.)*

TAREK. Where you from, Walter?

WALTER. Me? Oh, um, upstate New York.

TAREK. I heard it's pretty up there.

WALTER. Oh well...um, thank you.

(*Beat, as neither know what to say next.*)

Well, I don't want to interrupt your practicing.

TAREK. It won't bother you?

WALTER. No, it's fine.

TAREK. Great. Thanks. I'll keep my pants on.

WALTER. Oh even better.

(**TAREK***'s cell phone rings – he checks it.*)

TAREK. Ah – my mom. Calls every week to make sure I'm okay.

(**TAREK** *goes to the other room.* **WALTER** *sits, trying Tarek's drum. Hits it once or twice. Then again. And again. Closes his eyes as he finds some odd sort of almost-groove that is almost-recognizable. Opens his eyes and* **TAREK** *stands in front of him.*)

WALTER. Oh. Hi.

TAREK. Sounds good, Walter.

WALTER. I'm sorry.

TAREK. Don't be sorry, that's what it's there for. I heard you from the other room and I was like, "what's the crazy rhythm?"

WALTER. Jingle Bells.

TAREK. (*Takes out another drum and sits.*) Sit. Let me show you how. I'll show you how. Just put your feet flat on the ground. Now take the drum between your legs. Like this. Now you want to lift the inside edge off the ground with your ankles. Like this. Now, chest up, shoulders back. Feel relaxed? Great. Feel okay?

WALTER. Okay.

TAREK. Okay. Now, Walter, I know you're a very smart man but with the drum, it is not JUST about thinking, you have to feel it at the same time. Just thinking screws it up. Okay?

WALTER. Okay.

TAREK. Now just give it a couple of bangs.

(**WALTER** *hits a few, hard.*)

You're not angry at it.

WALTER. Oh. Right. Sorry.

(*He tries again.*)

TAREK. Better. Did you feel anything?

WALTER. I think so.

TAREK. Okay, now Walter, you listen to classical music, so you think in a very steady beat. One-two-three-four-one-two-three-four. Now this is an African drum, Walter, so you have to feel the syncopation, like a three inside of four.

[MUSIC NO. 05 – TWO AND THREE]

I had to learn to hear it too.

(**TAREK***'s drumming becomes music under, though the song is not at full feel yet.*)

LET GO THE FOUR AND THINK IN THREE –

COME, NOW, AND TRY WITH ME.

(*He drums a pattern and* **WALTER** *tries to follow by drumming on his chest. Quite badly.*)

Come on. Ta ta ta.

(**WALTER** *tries again. Better, still bad.*)

DON'T DO THE THING YOU THINK YOU SHOULD –
THINK OF THE THREE, NOW, THERE THAT'S GOOD!

> (**WALTER** *transfers his chest drumming back
> to the djembe.*)

Yeah! There it is. Okay. Good. You keep that up and
I will do this.

> (*He adds a rhythm, and that throws* **WALTER**
> *completely off.*)

Okay, okay, no problem. Back to this.

> (**TAREK** *returns to the first rhythm, and*
> **WALTER** *settles back in.*)

Now just feel that. Keep that going. There.

> (*He gently adds in the new rhythm. The song
> starts to build in feel.*)

TAKE UP THE SQUARE AND MAKE IT ROUND,
TASTE OF THE RHYTHM, TRY TO SEE THE SOUND.
DO EV'RYTHING YOU DON'T EXPECT –
DO WHAT'S RIGHT, NOT WHAT'S CORRECT.

I FEEL THAT YOU FEEL THE FRICTION NOW,
FINDING THE THREE WHERE THERE WERE TWO.
TRY LIVING WITH THE CONTRADICTION NOW –
DRUM OUT THE OLD AND HIT WHAT'S NEW.

WALK THE PARADE, BUT NOT IN STEP…
MAKE YOUR OWN RHYTHM, LET THE REST GET HEP.
THIS IS THE SOUND OF LIFE, THESE DRUMS:
THIS IS THE FABRIC LIFE BECOMES.

AND RHYTHM IS NOT A THING YOU FIND
RHYTHM IS NOT A THING YOU DO
NO, RHYTHM IS IN BODY, BREATH, AND MIND
FIND ALL YOU NEED INSIDE OF YOU.

TAREK.

> FEEL THE BEAT IN YOUR BLOOD...
> FEEL THE HIT IN YOUR HEART AND HAND...
> FIND THE RHYTHM WITHIN...
>
> SOON ENOUGH YOU WILL UNDERSTAND
> WHAT YOU NEVER CAN SAY...
> WHAT YOU ONLY CAN PLAY...
>
> JUST TAKE THAT TWO AND MAKE IT THREE,
> DO IT YOURSELF BUT RIGHT WITH ME, NOW,
> THAT'S THE SOUND OF LIFE YOU SEE –
> THE SOUND OF WHAT MIGHT BE
>
> BEAT BY BEAT I KNOW YOU FEEL THE FRICTION NOW,
> FINDING THE THREE WHERE THERE WERE TWO.
> YOU'RE LIVIN' IN THE CONTRADICTION NOW –
> DRUM OUT THE OLD AND HIT WHAT'S NEW.

WALTER.

> TWO NEEDS THREE AND THREE NEEDS TWO.

TAREK.

> ME AND YOU AND ME AND YOU.
> DRUM OUT THE OLD AND HIT WHAT'S NEW.

> (**TAREK**'s *cell phone rings again. He stops playing to check.*)

Oh-oh Walter. This might be an apartment. Excuse me.

(*As he is exiting.*) Yo, what's up, Rob?

> (*He goes into the next room.* **WALTER** *keeps playing. After a moment, he stands and removes his pants. Then sits and continues playing.* **ZAINAB** *enters, and* **WALTER** *stops, out of breath.*)

WALTER. Hello.

ZAINAB. Hello.

WALTER. Tarek is teaching me the drum.

ZAINAB. *(Re: the pants.)* Is Tarek home?

WALTER. Next room. On the phone.

ZAINAB. *(Starts into the next room, pauses.)* Please keep practicing. If you like.

> (**WALTER** *starts putting his pants back on.* **TAREK** *returns.)*

TAREK. Habibti. Rob hit me up, and I think we will have a place locked down by the end of the day, Inshallah.

ZAINAB. *(Relieved.)* Inshallah.

TAREK. How was your day?

ZAINAB. One clumsy tourist fell on my table and broke it. Worst of all, he didn't even buy anything!

TAREK. What, you didn't make him pay for the table?

> *(She looks at him with a "really?" face.)*

ZAINAB. Come on, now.

TAREK. I'd have chased him down the street.

ZAINAB. *(Re: his temper.)* That's 'cause you my dear, run too hot!

> (**TAREK** *has an idea.)*

TAREK. Hey Walter, what are you doing right now?

WALTER. Um!

TAREK. You are coming with me. Put your shoes on.

ZAINAB. I got to pick up a new table at five, I need you.

TAREK. It's only 2:30, I'll be back. Don't you worry, habibti.

ZAINAB. Don't habibti me!

TAREK. Come Walter, grab your drum.

WALTER. What does habibti mean?

TAREK. My beloved.

WALTER. Does she know that?

(*Pants on,* **WALTER** *follows* **TAREK** *out of the door.*)

(*Lights.*)

[MUSIC NO. 06 – DRUM CIRCLE]

(*Transition to:*)

(*Subway platform.*)

(**TAREK** *and* **WALTER** *wait. A* **DRUMMER** *plays opposite.*)

TAREK. This is King Taka. You are coming to the park, right? I always wanted to play down here, especially in the Times Square station. It's supposed to be amazing money.

WALTER. So why haven't you?

TAREK. Well – you need a permit.

WALTER. Of course.

(**WALTER** *watches as two* **POLICE OFFICERS** *stroll by.*)

TAREK. Maybe someday we can do it together. Split the profits.

WALTER. Why not?

(*They board a train.*)

(*One by one, other* **MUSICIANS** *join in with the* **DRUMMER** *as we transition to:*)

(Central Park.)

*(**MUSICIANS** enter, most with hand drums, a few with other instruments. They form a drum circle and begin playing.)*

*(**WALTER** and **TAREK** arrive.)*

TAREK. This is my friend Walter.

DRUMMER. Hey Walter, have a seat.

WALTER. I think I'll just watch.

*(**TAREK** sits and plays, finding the groove right away.)*

TAREK.
GIVE IT A TRY – JUST HIT THAT SIMPLE RHYTHM
GIVE IT A GO – YOU KNOW THIS – BOOM BOOM BOOM
YOU FEAR THAT YOU WON'T FIT
BUT ANYWHERE THAT YOU SIT THERE'S ROOM

*(**WALTER** sits and waits. Plays a few tentative hits.)*

LISTEN A WHILE AND THEN SOON YOU'LL FALL IN WITH 'EM
LISTEN A WHILE AND HEAR THAT HEARTBEAT POUND
SOON YOU'RE TAKING THE RIDE
SOON YOU'RE SLIPPING INSIDE THE SOUND

*(**WALTER** plays a few more hits. Slowly starts to find a rhythm.)*

YOU SLIP INTO THE CIRCLE
YOU SLIDE ALONG THE BEAT INSIDE THE BEAT
YOU STEP INTO THE CIRCLE
AND IT'S COMPLETE

*(**BYSTANDERS** in the park move to the music. The whole park gets involved.)*

(*A* **DRUMMER** *advises* **WALTER.**)

MALE DRUMMER.
WE'RE RIDING THE RHYTHM, IT'S NOT ABOUT
 PERFECTION
THAT NO ONE MAN CAN RULE – BUT ALL CONTROL

MALE DRUMMER & FEMALE DRUMMER.
JUST LEAVE YOUR EGO BEHIND
AND SHARE ONE HEART ONE MIND ONE SOUL

ANOTHER DRUMMER.	**ENSEMBLE.**
A BODY IN RHYTHM – IT'S ALL ABOUT CONNECTION	LA LA LA, LA LA LA LA LA LA, LA LA LA
REVEALING AND HEALING SO SIMPLE, SWEET AND PURE	LA LA LA, LA LA LA LA LA LA
SO OPEN THE HEART THAT AILS	OH
THE RHYTHM IT NEVER FAILS TO CURE	OH

CIRCLE (FULL ENSEMBLE).
AND SO YOU JOIN THE CIRCLE
AND SO YOU PLAY SO CLEAR SO TRUE
AND SO YOU JOIN THE CIRCLE
AND IT JOINS YOU

CIRCLE.
OH PLAY

JOIN THE CIRCLE FOR TOMORROW	**TAREK.**
	TRIP INTO THE CIRCLE RUN INTO THE CIRCLE AND PLAY
PLAY	
FIND THE BEAT AND PLAY FOR JOY	
	MOVE INTO THE CIRCLE
FOR NEED	

CIRCLE.
FOR LIGHT

TAREK & DRUMMER.
GROOVE INTO THE CIRCLE

**TAREK, DRUMMER &
ANOTHER DRUMMER.**
PROVE IT IN THE CIRCLE
ALL NIGHT

PLAY ALL NIGHT
ALL NIGHT

THAT'S HOW WE JOIN THE CIRCLE
THAT'S HOW WE MAKE OF MANY SONGS ONE SONG
THAT'S HOW WE JOIN THE CIRCLE
THAT'S HOW WE'RE STRONG

THAT'S HOW WE JOIN
THE CIRCLE

TAREK.
STEP INTO THE CIRCLE

THAT'S HOW YOU JOIN
YOUR HAND TO
EV'RY HAND
AND WHEN YOU JOIN
THE CIRCLE

EV'RY HAND
AND WHEN YOU JOIN
THE CIRCLE

TAREK.
YOU UNDERSTAND

CIRCLE.
YOU UNDERSTAND
OH OH OH, OH OH OH
OH OH OH, OH OH OH
OH OH OH, OH OH OH
OH OH OH, OH OH OH.

(Song segues. **TAREK** *stops drumming and
stands.)*

[MUSIC NO. 06A – THE ARREST]

TAREK. Shit! Walter.

WALTER. What!

TAREK. I have to go. Zainab is gonna kill me. She's waiting at the market!

WALTER. Oh – okay –

TAREK. I'm on Arab time again.

WALTER. Arab time? Can you say that?

TAREK. I can, but you can't. That was fun, right?

WALTER. My hands, they hurt.

TAREK. The more calluses the better. Here hold this.

WALTER. Okay...

> (**TAREK** *leaps over the turnstile – and is immediately approached by a* **TRANSIT COP.**)

TRANSIT COP #1. Hey!

TRANSIT COP #2. Are you fucking serious right now?

TAREK. What?

TRANSIT COP #1. Oh, come on, you just jumped!

TRANSIT COP #2. We saw you jump.

TAREK. No I paid. The drum moved the turnstile.

TRANSIT COP #1. The drum? That's a new one...

TRANSIT COP #2. You're kidding, right?

TAREK. No, check it out. Run my card. It will show you I paid.

WALTER. He paid, I saw him.

> (**TRANSIT COP #1** *puts up a hand to stop* **WALTER,** *takes out pad.*)

TRANSIT COP #1. Identification, sir.

TAREK. Why?

(**WALTER** *comes down, tries to intervene.*)

TRANSIT COP #1. Why? I'm writing you up! Show me an ID.

TAREK. Come on man, that don't make no sense.

(**WALTER** *steps in, downstage of* **TAREK**, *to intervene.*)

WALTER. Officer, this is a misunderstanding. I saw...

TRANSIT COP #1. Step back! Step back!

TRANSIT COP #2. *(Stepping in.)* Look, you show me an ID right now, or we're gonna have to take you in.

TAREK. And I said scan the card and it'll show you that you don't have to do any of this!

TRANSIT COP #2. Oh really? You gonna tell ME what to do! Come on.

(*He takes* **TAREK**'s *arm.*)

TAREK. *(Pulling away.)* No, no! Get your hands off me man...

TRANSIT COP #2. *(Grabbing* **TAREK**.*)* Hey!

TAREK. *(Struggling to get away.)* Let go of me! Walter!

TRANSIT COP #2. Goddamnit! Get on the ground!

(*He takes* **TAREK** *down, both* **OFFICERS** *cuff him.*)

TAREK. Hey! Get off! I paid!

WALTER. Officers, he paid! This is crazy!

(**TRANSIT COPS** *take* **TAREK** *away.*)

Where are you taking him? Where are you taking him? Hey! Hey! Hey!

(*Lights.*)

[MUSIC NO. 07 – TAREK AND ZAINAB (REPRISE)]

(Transition to:)

(Walter's apartment.)

WALTER. I don't understand why it escalated in the way it...

ZAINAB. He knows better than that! Why did he even respond?

WALTER. *(Overlapping.)* – I'm sure there's some misunderstanding. I made a statement at the station, they'll let him go –

ZAINAB. You don't understand.

WALTER. What don't I understand?

ZAINAB. We are not citizens, Walter...

WALTER. You're...? Tarek's from Michigan.

ZAINAB. He arrived there when he was very young. From Syria. We are undocumented.

WALTER. I did not know that...

ZAINAB. Why would you know that?

WALTER. What can I do?

ZAINAB. What makes you think you can *do* anything?

WALTER. *(Slightly taken aback.)* Ummmm. Because... Maybe I'll call the precinct, find out what's happening.

> *(**WALTER** pulls out his cell phone and dials. He steps into the next room.)*

ZAINAB.
AMERICA MAKES THIS PROMISE
AMERICA KILLS YOUR DREAM.
HOW COULD YOU MAKE ME BELIEVE?

(*She breaks off.*)

Damn you, Tarek!

(**WALTER** *returns.*)

WALTER. They let him go but ICE picked him up.

ZAINAB. Of course they did.

WALTER. They've taken him... They've taken him to Queens.

(**ZAINAB** *sighs.*)

We aren't going to see him for a while.

ZAINAB. I can't visit him in that place or I will end up there, too.

(*Beat.*)

WALTER. I'll find an immigration attorney.

ZAINAB. We can't afford that.

WALTER. You don't have to worry about that.

ZAINAB. (*Snapping.*) Yes I do!

(*A beat.* **WALTER** *is taken aback slightly by this.*)

(*She has no idea how.*) I will find the way to pay you back...okay?

WALTER. Okay.

ZAINAB. I have a cousin in the Bronx. I will stay with him.

WALTER. You don't have to leave. You can stay here.

(*She snaps back almost automatically.*)

ZAINAB. (*Firm.*) That is not the way I intend to pay!

WALTER. I absolutely was not, in any way insinuating...

ZAINAB. Really? ...Don't tell me, I must trust you?

WALTER. Yes, you should trust me.

(**ZAINAB** *stares at him in disbelief.*)

ZAINAB. Do you think that is the first time I've heard that? I was in detention when I first arrived. The guards – the rats. Broken toilets. I was there five months.

WALTER. And you got out?

ZAINAB. They closed the facility and released some of the women. They didn't release any of the men.

WALTER. Zainab – I can't begin to imagine what you've been through.

[MUSIC NO. 08 – ZAINAB'S SONG (BOUND FOR AMERICA)]

ZAINAB. No. You can't.

TWELVE HUNDRED MILES IN A ONE-ENGINE PIROGUE
WE SET SAIL FROM PORT SAINT LOUIS
IN TWELVE TRYING DAYS, WE MADE LOS CRISTIANOS
STARVING AND SICK FROM THE SEA.

WITH FIVE DAYS NO WATER, AND THREE DAYS SINCE RAIN
SOME DRANK FROM THE SEA, WHICH PLAYED TRICKS ON
    THE BRAIN,
WITH SORES FROM WET CLOTHING, WITH FEVER, IN PAIN,
MOST WERE JUST HAPPY THEY DROPPED US IN SPAIN.

BUT ME, I WAS BOUND FOR AMERICA
ME, I WAS BOUND FOR AMERICA.

THEY LEFT US, NO PAPERS, TO ROAM BARCELONA
BUT I TOOK THE FIRST TRAIN TO FRANCE
STAYED WITH SOME COUSINS IN NICE
BEFORE CROSSING THE CHANNEL WHEN I HAD THE
    CHANCE

A NIGHT BOAT, LE HAVRE TO PORTSMOUTH, AT DAWN
THE MONEY MY FATHER HAD GIVEN ME, GONE

I WORKED FOR FIVE WEEKS 'TIL A CREW FROM TAIWAN
SHARED WORD OF A SHIP THEY COULD HELP ME GET ON

AT LAST, I WAS BOUND FOR AMERICA
NOW I WAS BOUND FOR AMERICA

BUT THE PRICE OF THE VOYAGE WAS STEEP
THEY WOULD TOUCH ME WHEN I WAS ASLEEP
SO I TOOK TO LONG NIGHTS UP ON DECK
THEN THEY PUT ME AGROUND IN QUEBEC
BUT ONE SAILOR, HE KNEW A BOSS
WHO FOR A PRICE WOULD HELP ME ACROSS
BUT I HAD JUST PENNIES, OR LESS
SO THE PRICE, BY THIS POINT, I COULD GUESS…

  (This hangs there. Then:)

WALTER. Zainab, I'm so sorry.

ZAINAB. You have no reason to be.

WALTER. Can I at least call a car for you?

ZAINAB. Please don't. What you are doing for Tarek is enough.

WALTER. I'll find an attorney, and I'll go see Ta… Damn – I have to give a paper in the afternoon, but I'll go see Tarek right after.

  *(**WALTER** goes.)*

ZAINAB.
 A PIROGUE FROM SENEGAL TO TENERIFE
 TO FAM'LY IN FRANCE WHERE MY RESPITE WAS BRIEF
 TO CROSSINGS THAT COST UNACCOUNTABLE GRIEF
 THIS LAND IS MY FORTUNE, THE JOURNEY'S A THIEF

 BUT HERE I AM, NOW, IN AMERICA
 AT LEAST, AND FOR NOW, IN AMERICA.

  (Lights.)

[MUSIC NO. 09 – HERE IN THE FIRST WORLD]

(Transition to:)

(Hotel Ballroom.)

*(**ECONOMISTS** gather, chattering among themselves. **WALTER** enters, looks at them and they all begin to move in rhythm.)*

*(One approaches **WALTER**.)*

ECONOMIST. Walter, I'm looking forward to your paper.

WALTER. Well, it's not really my paper.

ECONOMIST. *(Overlaps.)* I've been thinking quite a bit about incorporating some notion of infrastructure advancement into my own research.

CONFERENCE CHAIR. Welcome to day three of NYU's economic forum. Please welcome from Connecticut College, Dr. Walter Vale, who will read his paper on ramifications of moral hazard in microfinance.

WALTER. It's not really my paper. Three decades of investment in microfinance have eased liquidity constraints for millions of low-wealth people around the developing world. Low-wealth people?

(Interrupting himself:)

HERE IN THE FIRST WORLD
THE SUNRISE RISES ROSY
WE DRINK COFFEE IN A COZY IN OUR CAR
LEARNING FACTS FROM NPR

However, in the act of lending to people who possibly cannot repay, the moral hazard that results is not inconsequential...

HERE IN THE FIRST WORLD
WE LOVE TO HAVE OUR THEORIES
HYPOTHESES AND QUERIES
STAY ABSTRACT
DO ANYTHING BUT ACT.

AND WE STRAIN TO HEAR A DISTANT, THRUMMING DRUM
AND WE STAND TO SING AND FIND WE'VE BEEN STRUCK
    DUMB

AND WE WAIT FOR REVOLUTIONS THAT WON'T COME
HERE IN THE FIRST WORLD
HERE IN THE FIRST –

    (**ALL** *foot stomp.*)

Given that small loan sizes make it expensive to monitor borrowers.

TODAY IN THE FIRST WORLD
WE DROWN IN INFORMATION
THE MOST ENLIGHTENED NATION
ARE WE LOST,
AND JUST COUNTING UP THE COST?

HERE IN THE FIRST WORLD
WE LIVE OUR LIVES OF WONDER
WE DON'T LISTEN TO THE THUNDER
FAR AWAY
THERE'S ONLY SUN TODAY

AND WE DEIGN TO DANCE ON FEET OF DRIEST CLAY
AND WE BURN TO RUN BUT KNOW WE'LL ALWAYS STAY
FOR WE'RE SURE THE EARTH WILL EVER SPIN OUR WAY
HERE IN THE FIRST WORLD
HERE IN THE FIRST WORLD

    (*He turns and finds* **TAREK** *playing his drum.*)

A FEW DJEMBE LESSONS AND LIKE THAT I AM
    ENLIGHTENED

WALTER.
MY CONSCIENCE IS AWAKENED,
MY SENSE OF GRIEVANCE HEIGHTENED
ONE IMMIGRANT I BARELY KNOW IS SUDDENLY IN
DANGER
AND INSTANTLY I THINK I KNOW THE PLIGHT OF EV'RY
STRANGER

I'M SUDDENLY AWARE
I SAY ANOTHER PRAYER
FOR ANOTHER MAN'S DESPAIR

ECONOMISTS GROUP 1.
WE SHOW WE CARE...

ECONOMISTS GROUP 2.
SHOW WE CARE...

WALTER & ECONOMISTS GROUP 3.
SHOW WE CARE...

ECONOMISTS GROUP 1.
WE SHOW WE CARE...

ECONOMISTS GROUP 2.
SHOW WE CARE...

WALTER & ECONOMISTS GROUP 3.
SHOW WE CARE...

ALL ECONOMISTS.
SHOW WE

WALTER & ECONOMISTS GROUP 3.
SHOW

ECONOMISTS GROUP 1.
SHOW

ECONOMISTS GROUP 2.
SHOW

WALTER & ALL ECONOMISTS.
OH

(The **ECONOMISTS** *jump up and join in and dance and drum and go nuts.)*

WALTER.

WE'VE CONQUERED
  FAMINE, WAR, DISEASE,
  AND DROUGHT

ALONG WITH ANY TRACE
  OF MORAL DOUBT

LIKE THE OUTSIDE WORLD,
  WE'VE LEARNED TO
  KEEP IT OUT
OUT OF THE FIRST WORLD

BUT WE STRAIN TO
  HEAR A DISTANT,
  THRUMMING DRUM

AND WE STAND TO SING
  AND FIND WE'VE BEEN
  STRUCK DUMB

AND WE WAIT FOR
  REVOLUTIONS THAT
  WON'T COME
HERE IN THE FIRST WORLD

HERE IN THE FIRST WORLD

ECONOMISTS.

WE'VE CONQUERED –

CONQUERED FAMINE,
  WAR, DISEASE, AND
  DROUGHT

ALONG WITH ANY TRACE
  OF MORAL DOUBT

AHH

OUT OF THE FIRST WORLD
OUT OF THE FIRST WORLD

LA LA LA LA LA LA LA LA LA
AHH

LA LA LA LA LA LA LA LA LA
AHH

THEY WON'T COME

HERE IN THE FIRST WORLD
OH

ECONOMISTS. *(Variously.)*

NO MORE BUILDING NATIONS

WALTER.

HERE IN THE FIRST WORLD

ECONOMISTS.

HERE IN THE FIRST
JUST THINK TANKS AND FOUNDATIONS

WALTER.

HERE IN THE FIRST WORLD

ECONOMISTS.

HERE IN THE FIRST WORLD

WALTER & ECONOMISTS.

CAUTIOUS WITH CONVICTION
HERE IN THE FIRST WORLD

PRIV'LEGE IS AFFLICTION
HERE IN THE FIRST WORLD

I SAID

WALTER.

HERE	**ECONOMISTS.**
	HERE!
HERE	
	HERE!
HERE	
	HERE!
HERE	
	HERE!

WALTER & ECONOMISTS.

HERE IN THE FIRST WORLD!

(On the final chord, all the **ECONOMISTS** *drop into their seats as if they hadn't just been dancing.)*

*(***WALTER** *is at the lectern, finishing reading the paper.* **ZAINAB** *is looking in his direction.)*

To conclude, these must be business decisions. It's imperative for the success of future microfinance that we reject any shared responsibility for moral hazard.

(Looks up.)

Although – I don't know if it's ever a good idea to reject shared responsibility –

(Catches himself.)

– but I suppose I should take that up with my co-author. For another time. Thank you.

(He gets polite applause from the **ECONOMISTS** *and exits.)*

(Lights.)

[MUSIC NO. 10 – ZAINAB'S LETTER]

*(***ZAINAB*** *is in a spot, composing a letter.)*

ZAINAB. Dearest Tarek. I hope that you're well.

KNOW THAT THAT PLACE WILL NOT BE FOREVER
TAKE IT ALL DAY BY DAY
TAREK, I WILL SEE YOU SOON – SOME WAY

JE T'AIME
JE T'AIME

(Detention Center.)

*(***WALTER*** *is sitting on one side of a plexiglass partition, opposite* **TAREK**, *who wears an inmate's uniform of a dark-blue shirt and pants.)*

*(***WALTER*** *is pressing the letter against the glass so* **TAREK** *can read.)*

TAREK. Thank you, Walter.

WALTER. How are you, how are you holding up?

TAREK. Not well. Have you seen Zainab?

WALTER. She's doing fine.

TAREK. So what did your lawyers say exactly?

WALTER. Were you and your mother denied asylum?

TAREK. Yes. But we appealed.

WALTER. Did you have a deportation hearing?

TAREK. We did everything they told us to.

WALTER. But there's a final deportation order out on you? If they reopen the case, they're going to deport you.

> *(Beat.)*

Maybe you should call your mother.

TAREK. No!

WALTER. She might have information that could help.

TAREK. No!

WALTER. But Tarek –

TAREK. I don't want to worry her.

WALTER. But if you're deported.

TAREK. This is crazy!

[MUSIC NO. 11 – WORLD BETWEEN TWO WORLDS]

They treat us like criminals. I'm not a criminal.

THEY CUFF OUR HANDS AND CHAIN OUR FEET
THEY GIVE US SOAP BUT CRAP TO EAT
AND ONE HARD COT WITH ONE GREY SHEET
AND THIS UNIFORM – THAT'S ALL.

THEY LET US OUT AN HOUR FOR AIR
NO PLACE TO READ, NO RUGS FOR PRAYER
JUST HOURS ON END TO SIT AND STARE
AT THE FACELESS CONCRETE WALL

AND MANY MEN ARE STUCK INSIDE FOR WELL MORE
    THAN A YEAR
BUT I'D GO CRAZY WALTER – GET ME OUT OF HERE

OUT OF THIS
WORLD BETWEEN TWO WORLDS
THIS HOME FOR MEN WITH NONE
THE LIGHTS STAY ON ALL NIGHT
SO DAYS ARE NEVER DONE.

WALTER. My lawyer's on the case. Please. Don't worry.

TAREK.

I'M TERRIFIED, I CAN'T PRETEND
BUT YOU'VE BEEN SUCH A FAITHFUL FRIEND
WE'LL SEE THIS THROUGH, UNTIL THE END
TELL ZAINAB NOT TO FEAR.

WALTER. Of course.

TAREK.

I'LL MAKE IT OUT, BUT GOD KNOWS WHEN
SO HELP HER TO STAY STRONG 'TIL THEN
AND PROMISE ME YOU'LL COME AGAIN
DON'T FORGET ME HERE.

WALTER.

I WON'T FORGET YOU HERE

TAREK.

DON'T FORGET ME HERE

WALTER.

HERE

TAREK.

HERE

WALTER.

HERE

WALTER & TAREK.
IN THIS
WORLD BETWEEN TWO WORLDS

TAREK.
THIS WAREHOUSE FULL OF SOULS
THIS JAIL THAT'S NOT A JAIL
THAT NO GOVERNMENT CONTROLS
WHERE NIGHTS ARE FREEZING COLD
AND GUARDS RUN MEAN AND HOT
IN THIS WORLD BETWEEN TWO WORLDS

WALTER.
WORLD BETWEEN TWO WORLDS

TAREK.
WHERE EV'RY DAY'S THE SAME UNTIL IT'S NOT.

(A **GUARD** *intercedes and lifts* **TAREK** *out of his chair.)*

GUARD. All right, that's enough. Let's go.

TAREK. *(As the* **GUARD** *drags him away.)*
DON'T FORGET ME HERE, WALTER

WALTER.
I WON'T, TAREK.

TAREK.
DON'T FORGET OUR DRUMS

WALTER.
I WON'T.

TAREK.
WE'LL PLAY TOGETHER SOON, WALTER
WHATEVER COMES

(As the **GUARD** *drags* **TAREK** *out:)*

WALTER. We will, Tarek. We will.

(Lights.)

(Elsewhere in the detention center, the **DETAINEES** *are being lined up.* **TAREK** *is brought to join them.)*

DETAINEES.	TAREK.

DETAINEES.
DON'T FORGET ME HERE, DAUGHTER
DON'T FORGET ME, WIFE
WE'LL BE TOGETHER SOON, MY SON
AND BACK TO LIFE

TAREK.
DON'T LEAVE ME HERE ALONE
DON'T LEAVE ME LOCKED AWAY

(Meanwhile, **WALTER** *moves to the street.)*

TAREK.
BACK TO LIFE

TAREK & DETAINEES.
BACK TO LIFE
OUT
OF
THIS
WORLD BETWEEN TWO WORLDS
THIS HOME FOR MEN WITH NONE
THE LIGHTS STAY ON ALL NIGHT
SO DAYS ARE NEVER DONE

THE NIGHTS ARE FREEZING COLD
THE BRUTAL GUARDS RUN HOT
IN THIS WORLD BETWEEN TWO WORLDS

WHERE EV'RY DAY'S THE SAME...
EV'RY DAY'S THE SAME...
EV'RY DAY'S THE SAME...

(One **DETAINEE** *disappears.)*

*(***TAREK** *stares at the spot where he was standing.* **WALTER**, *opposite, stares at* **TAREK**.*)*

TAREK.
UNTIL IT'S NOT.

(A detention door slams shut.)

(Lights.)

End of Act One

ACT TWO

[MUSIC NO. 12 – ENTR'ACTE]

(As the Entr'acte begins to fade, lights up on Walter's apartment.)

*(**WALTER** is practicing the djembe.)*

(A knock at the door.)

*(He pulls on his pants and opens the door to **MOUNA**.)*

WALTER. Hello.

MOUNA. I'm sorry. I must have the wrong apartment.

WALTER. Can I help you?

MOUNA. I'm looking for my son. Excuse me.

WALTER. Are you Tarek's mother?

MOUNA. Yes.

WALTER. Oh. This is Tarek's apartment. I – share the apartment with him. Please.

MOUNA. He did not mention that he lived with someone.

WALTER. I'm not here very often. I live in Connecticut.

MOUNA. Is Tarek here?

WALTER. No. He's – ah – he's not here now.

MOUNA. I'll come back. When might you expect him?

WALTER. Mrs. –

MOUNA. Khalil. Mouna Khalil.

WALTER. My name is Walter. Walter Vale. Please sit down.

(A moment, and **MOUNA** *follows* **WALTER** *into the apartment.)*

Can I get you some water?

MOUNA. No, I'm fine. Mr. Vale...

WALTER. Your son is in an immigration detention center. We were in the subway. The police grabbed him.

MOUNA. I knew something was wrong when I didn't hear from him. How long has he been there?

WALTER. About ten days. We got him a lawyer.

MOUNA. Really? And how long did this lawyer say he'd be in there?

WALTER. Difficult to predict. Forgive the intrusion, Mrs. Khalil, but do you remember your asylum hearing?

MOUNA. I do.

WALTER. What happened after?

MOUNA. We appealed.

WALTER. And the appeal was denied?

MOUNA. Yes.

WALTER. And they sent you a letter that told you where to show up and be deported?

MOUNA. No.

WALTER. You never received that letter? The lawyer says that happens sometimes. But if you got the letter and ignored it, there's nothing the lawyer can do.

MOUNA. We didn't get a letter.

WALTER. Okay.

MOUNA. So what does the lawyer say?

WALTER. He's filing for an emergency stay. He says it's difficult – things are very black and white now. But this will help.

MOUNA. I see. Can you put me in touch with this lawyer?

WALTER. First thing tomorrow.

MOUNA. Very well, then. Thank you.

>   *(She stands to go.)*

WALTER. But where will you go?

MOUNA. I will find a hotel.

WALTER. You can stay here.

MOUNA. Thank you for your offer. I don't want to impose.

WALTER. You're not imposing.

>   *(Beat.)*

You can use Tarek's room. It's here.

[MUSIC NO. 13 – WHAT LITTLE I CAN DO (PREPRISE)]

Please, I would like you to stay.

MOUNA. Again, thank you, however…

WALTER. Mrs. Khalil –

YOUR TAREK WAS WITH ME, YOU SEE
THE TRAIN, THE DAY THAT HE WAS CAUGHT.
YOUR SON HAS BEEN A FRIEND TO ME.
I PROMISED THAT I'D HELP HIM, AS I OUGHT.

>   *(**MOUNA** heads to the space, looks into the room. Feels the spirit of her son.)*

WALTER.
   I WISH YOU'D LET ME HELP AS WELL.
   A HOME,
   AND NOT A COLD HOTEL
   MORE COMFORTABLE, MORE FRIENDLY, TOO
   I WISH YOU'D LET ME DO
   WHAT LITTLE I CAN DO

MOUNA. All right. Thank you, Mr. Vale.

WALTER. Great. Please. Call me Walter.

MOUNA. Then you'll call me Mouna.

WALTER. All right. Mouna.

MOUNA. I would like to go there. To the detention center. Now.

WALTER. Okay – Are you sure you –

MOUNA. I won't go in. I just want to see where they are holding him.

WALTER.
   THEY'LL LET ME BRING A NOTE INSIDE –

MOUNA.
   AND NOTHING MORE?

WALTER.
   NO, I'VE TRIED.
   BUT THAT WILL MEAN THE WORLD, IT'S TRUE –
   AT TIMES LIKE THIS, WE DO
   WHAT LITTLE WE CAN DO

MOUNA. *(Seeing the drums.)* Tarek wanted to come to New York to play music. I told him not to come.

WALTER. I'll get my coat.

   (He goes. **MOUNA** *gently taps a drum.)*

MOUNA.

MY SON, I'M NOT SURE WHY I CAME
THEY MAY DEPORT YOU JUST THE SAME,
AND WHY MY SON? I WISH I KNEW –

WELL, NOW I'M HERE, I'LL DO
WHAT LITTLE I CAN DO…
WHAT LITTLE I CAN DO…

(Lights.)

(The Detention Center. Again, **WALTER** *is led to the cubicle where* **TAREK** *waits.)*

TAREK. My mother is here?! Where?

WALTER. She's waiting across the street – at a diner.

TAREK. Oh, man. Why did she come? Walter, tell her I said she has to go back to Michigan.

WALTER. Okay. She sent a letter.

[MUSIC NO. 14 – WHERE IS HOME? / NO HOME]

(He holds the letter up to the glass. **TAREK** *reads it.)*

MOUNA.

MY DEAREST TAREK.
ARE YOU HEALTHY IN THERE?
ARE YOU SLEEPING ALL RIGHT?
I THINK OF YOU NIGHT AND NOON
WE'LL HAVE YOU HOME SOON…

TAREK.

BUT WHERE IS HOME?
IS IT NEW YORK?
OR IS IT MICHIGAN?
IS IT ANN ARBOR,

TAREK.
> WHERE THE WINTER TREES AT LAST ARE SHOWING
>   BUDS AGAIN

MOUNA & TAREK.
> THE BIRDS ARE BACK TO SING, THE RIVER FLOODS AGAIN.
> DO YOU THINK OF THIS?
> IS THAT THE PLACE YOU MISS
> WHEN DAYS ARE DONE?

MOUNA.
> WHERE IS HOME,
> MY SON?

> *(Lights.)*

> *(A diner.* **MOUNA** *sits alone, drinking tea.)*

NASIM. Darjeeling, Miss. May I offer you anything else? Something to eat?

MOUNA. No, thank you.

> *(Two* **GUARDS** *sit in an adjacent booth. She stares at them. Another two Detention Center* **GUARDS** *almost push the waiter,* **NASIM,** *aside and sit at a table.)*

GUARD. Two coffees.

NASIM. *(Under his breath.)* Two coffees please.

GUARD. What was that?

NASIM. Two coffees, right away, sir.

> *(***MOUNA** *also considers the* **GUARDS.***)*

MOUNA.
> THOSE MEN WITH THEIR BADGES, THEIR CURSES,
>   THEIR GUNS
> THESE MEN MUST HAVE FATHERS AND BROTHERS AND
>   SONS

IF THEY ARE AMERICA, WHAT THEN OF ME?
I HAVE MORE IN COMMON WITH THE BOY WHO SERVES
   TEA.

(Split scene:)

(Lights on **TAREK**, *back in his cell.)*

*(***OTHER DETAINEES*** around him.)*

AND STILL I WONDER
WERE WE RIGHT TO HAVE STAYED?
BUT WHAT ELSE COULD WE DO?
THE HOME THAT WE KNEW IS AT WAR
AND WORSE THAN BEFORE.

NOW WHERE IS HOME?

TAREK.
   WHERE IS HOME?

MOUNA.
   IT'S NOT NEW YORK.

TAREK.
   IT'S NOT NEW YORK.

MOUNA.
   IT ISN'T SYRIA.

NASIM.
   ALEXANDRIA

TAREK.
   IS IT ANN ARBOR?

MOUNA & TAREK.	**NASIM.**
WHERE THE WINTER TREES AT LAST ARE SHOWING BUDS AGAIN.	AHH
THE BIRDS ARE BACK TO SING, THE RIVER FLOODS AGAIN.	AHH

NASIM.
THE MULBERRY FLOWERS...

MOUNA, TAREK & NASIM.
BUT WAS IT EVER OURS?

MOUNA & TAREK.
HOW COULD IT BE?
WHERE IS HOME
WHERE IS HOME
FOR YOU AND ME?

(**WALTER** *enters the diner.*)

MOUNA. How is he?

WALTER. He's good – but he's concerned about your being in New York.

MOUNA. Tell him I cannot go back to Michigan knowing that he is in that building. Even if I can't see him, I will stay.

WALTER. All right.

TAREK.
WHERE IS HOME?

MOUNA. And Walter – I should like to meet Zainab.

WALTER. You've never met?

MOUNA. No. I did not approve of their dating.

WALTER. Because...

MOUNA. Because she also is undocumented.

TAREK.
WHERE IS HOME?

(**MOUNA** *reaches for her pocketbook.*)

NASIM. The tea is on me.

MOUNA. Thank you. That's very kind.

(**WALTER** *and* **MOUNA** *go.*)

TAREK.
WHERE IS HOME
FOR YOU AND ME?

ONE DETAINEE.
THIS IS NO HOME

TAREK.
WHERE IS HOME?

THREE DETAINEES.
THIS IS NO HOME
NO HOME

TAREK.
WHERE IS HOME?

SIX DETAINEES.
NO HOME

TAREK.
WHERE IS HOME
FOR YOU AND ME?

ALL DETAINEES.
THIS IS NO HOME

TAREK.
WHERE IS HOME?

ALL DETAINEES.
THIS IS NO HOME
NO HOME

TAREK.
WHERE IS HOME?

ALL DETAINEES.
NO HOME

TAREK.

WHERE IS HOME

ALL DETAINEES.

NO HOME

TAREK & DETAINEES.

FOR YOU AND ME?

> *(The* **DETAINEES** *grow restless, raising their voices, stomping their feet, drowning* **TAREK** *out.)*

TAREK.

THIS IS NO HOME

ALL DETAINEES.

NO HOME!

TAREK.

THIS IS NO HOME

ALL DETAINEES.

NO HOME AHH

TAREK.

THIS IS NO HOME

ALL DETAINEES.

NO HOME!

TAREK.

THIS IS NO HOME

ALL DETAINEES.

NO HOME AHH!

TAREK & TWO DETAINEES.

NO HOME NO HOME

OTHER DETAINEES.

NO HOME!

TAREK & TWO DETAINEES.
NO HOME NO HOME

OTHER DETAINEES.
NO HOME!

TAREK & TWO DETAINEES.
NO HOME NO HOME

OTHER DETAINEES.
NO HOME!

TAREK & TWO DETAINEES.
NO HOME NO HOME

OTHER DETAINEES.
NO HOME!

(**ONE DETAINEE** *becomes very animated.*)

ONE DETAINEE.
SAY –

OTHER DETAINEES.
NO HOME

ONE DETAINEE.
HEY –

OTHER DETAINEES.
NO HOME

ALL.
NO – NO –

TAREK & ONE DETAINEE.
SAY –

OTHER DETAINEES.
NO HOME!

(*A* **GUARD** *rushes in.*)

GUARD. Lights out! That's enough!

ONE DETAINEE.
SAY –

OTHER DETAINEES.
NO HOME

ONE DETAINEE.
HEY –

OTHER DETAINEES.
NO HOME

ALL.
NO – NO –

TAREK & ONE DETAINEE.
SAY –

OTHER DETAINEES.
NO HOME

> *(The **GUARD** raises his club to strike the detainee, but **TAREK** intercedes.)*

TAREK. No – don't – he's just angry – he's not going to do anything –

ALL DETAINEES.
NO HOME
NO HOME

> *(The club comes down on **TAREK**.)*

GUARD. Lights out. Now.

> *(The **GUARD** goes as **TAREK** painfully lifts himself to a sitting position.)*

TAREK.
THERE WILL BE HOME...
SOMEHOW, YOU'LL SEE...
WE WILL FIND HOME
FOR YOU AND ME.

(Two of the **OTHER DETAINEES** *help* **TAREK** *up and away.)*

(Lights.)

(Transition to:)

(Staten Island Ferry.)

*(***MOUNA** *and* **ZAINAB** *draw their light jackets or sweaters against the stiff spring breeze on deck.)*

ZAINAB. ...I thought it might be better to talk here. The market is very... I'm sorry I reacted like that.

MOUNA. It's fine.

ZAINAB. I don't normally burst into tears, just...

(Beat as she gently, sub-textually speaks her truth.)

Us – never really having spoken. I didn't know what to expect.

*(***MOUNA** *hears the subtext loud and clear.)*

MOUNA. And now that we've met, am I what you imagined?

ZAINAB. Are we ever?

(Beat.)

It's very cold out here, would you like to go back inside?

MOUNA. No, I'm fine.

ZAINAB. I'm still not accustomed to it.

MOUNA. Do you miss...Senegal?

ZAINAB. Yes. But I don't want to live there. Do you miss Syria?

MOUNA. My heart breaks for it. But this is home now.

ZAINAB. That's exactly what Tarek would say each time we moved. "This is home now" ...I don't know what to do, I miss him so much.

MOUNA. Would you tell me more about you and Tarek?

ZAINAB. *(Glint of playful cheekiness in her eyes.)* Oh, now you want to know about us, eh?

>　　　*(Beat as* **MOUNA** *smiles in recognition of the truth.)*

MOUNA. It was not personal, Zainab. I wanted him to marry... So he could be safe... I'm sorry if I hurt you.

[MUSIC NO. 15 – LADY LIBERTY]

>　　　*(***ZAINAB*** smiles, her acceptance is in the tone of her reply.)*

ZAINAB. Tarek and I would jump onto this ferry all of the time. It felt like we were going somewhere. And it was free. And when he saw the Statue over there he'd come right up to the rail – *(As she does.)* – and point and shout. *(As she does.)* "Lady Liberty! Lady Liberty! There she is."

MOUNA. With different accents?

ZAINAB. So many accents. As if he, personally, had come from every corner of globe.

MOUNA. That sounds like my son. Always the actor.

ZAINAB. Always the life of the party.

>　　　*(***MOUNA*** stares at the statue, almost getting lost in it.)*

MOUNA. Funny, this close, she looks smaller than I thought. No? Can you imagine all she's seen? The hopes that faded on sight of her?

HEY LIBERTY LADY, STATUESQUE LADY
WHAT DO YOU HIDE IN THAT ROBE?
ORPHANS FROM OVER THE GLOBE?
THEY TUG AT YOUR HEM –
WHAT CAN YOU DO NOW FOR THEM?
YOU SAY GIVE ME YOUR TIRED, YOUR POOR,
WELL, WE'VE GOT MORE.
THEY KNOCK, BUT YOU'RE NOT AT THE DOOR.

ZAINAB.

HEY LIBERTY WOMAN, SERIOUS WOMAN,
UNDER THAT OPULENT CROWN,
AFTER THE TOWERS CAME DOWN
THEY CLOSED YOU UP FAST.
PUT OUT YOUR TORCHLIGHT AT LAST.
AND YOUR CROWN WAS OFF-LIMITS FOR YEARS.
LOST TO OUR FEARS.
IT STILL IS, OR SO IT APPEARS.

MOUNA.

LISTEN MISS LIBERTY, DON'T HEAR ME WRONG
YOU SURE DESERVE A VACATION
AFTER TWO OR THREE CENTURIES, STANDING THAT LONG
HOLDING THE HOPES OF A NATION

ZAINAB.

LISTEN, MISS LIBERTY, GO HAVE YOUR FUN –
BUT PLEASE LADY, PLEASE, DO COME BACK WHEN YOU'RE
    DONE

MOUNA & ZAINAB.

WE NEED YOU HERE
IT'S CLEAR

MOUNA.

HEY STATUE OF LIBERTY, TIRELESS LADY,
WE'RE WOMEN WHO WORK HARD LIKE YOU
WHEN WILL OUR TRIALS BE THROUGH?

MOUNA.
JUST GIVE US SOME WORD –
SWEAR THAT OUR PRAYER WILL BE HEARD

ZAINAB.
WE HAVE ALWAYS BELIEVED WHAT YOU SAY
THAT'S WHY WE STAY
AND LIBERTY LADY

MOUNA.
STATUESQUE LADY

ZAINAB.
FUN-LOVING LADY

MOUNA & ZAINAB.
OUR LONG-LOST LADY
WE BELIEVE YOU'LL BE BACK HERE, SOME DAY.
WE BELIEVE YOU'LL BE BACK HERE, SOME DAY.

[MUSIC NO. 15A – DETENTION CENTER 1]

(Lights.)

(Detention Center.)

*(***TAREK*** and ***WALTER***. **WALTER** *can see the bruise on* **TAREK**'s *head but tries not to ask about it.)*

TAREK. They went on the ferry?

WALTER. Yes.

TAREK. And they seemed to get along? Zainab and my mother?

WALTER. Yes. I think your mother likes her very much. Are you sure you're okay?

TAREK. I'm fine. Why is she still here? Did you tell her to go?

WALTER. I tried, but she won't go. She's worried.

TAREK. She's worried that I'll end up like my dad.

WALTER. Your dad?

TAREK. The government put him in jail for something he wrote. By the time they released him… He was dead within weeks. She doesn't want me to end up like him.

*(**TAREK** gently references his bruise.)*

WALTER. We're going to get you out. Tarek. Don't give up.

TAREK. Hey, you've been practicing?

WALTER. Yes, every day!

TAREK. Show me.

WALTER. *(Begins to drum in the cubicle.)* Hear that? How good is that?

TAREK. Well…

WALTER. *(Still drumming.)* I have a hard time keeping rhythm when I play alone.

TAREK. Because you're overthinking again, aren't you?

WALTER. I think so.

[MUSIC NO. 16 – HEART IN YOUR HANDS]

TAREK.
> DON'T FORCE IT, WALTER, FIND IT –
> DON'T FALL TOO FAR BEHIND IT –
> THERE, NOW, THAT'S THE WAY.
> NOW PROMISE ME YOU'LL PRACTICE –
> TWO HOURS AT LEAST OF PRACTICE,
> EV'RY DAY
> AND WHEN YOU GET ME FREE
> WE'LL PLAY
> WE'LL PLAY

TAREK.

JUST HEAR YOUR HEART
JUST FEEL YOUR HEART
JUST PUT YOUR HEART INTO YOUR HANDS AND PLAY
NOW ONE-TWO-THREE AS IF WITH ME

GUARD. All right, time's up. Let's go.

(A **GUARD** *pulls* **TAREK** *away.)*

TAREK.

YOU PUT YOUR HEART INTO YOUR HANDS AND PLAY

ENSEMBLE.

(Variously.) OOH
AHH

TAREK.

FORGET WHAT SOME ARE SAYING,
KEEP TRYING, MAN, KEEP PLAYING,
DON'T GIVE UP THE BEAT.

TAREK.	**ENSEMBLE.** *(Variously.)*
LET WORRIES STAY UNSPOKEN.	OOH
WE'RE BLOODIED BUT UNBROKEN –	OOH
ON OUR FEET.	OOH
AND WHEN I'M FREE WE'LL BE	WE'LL BE...
COMPLETE.	WE'LL BE...
COMPLETE	WE'LL BE...
JUST PUT YOUR HEART	AHH
JUST PUT YOUR HEART	AHH
JUST PUT YOUR HEART INTO YOUR HANDS AND PLAY	HEART HANDS AND AND PLAY

AN EASY ART, — AHH
WHILE WE'RE APART, — AHH
TO PUT YOUR HEART INTO — OOH
    YOUR HANDS AND PLAY.

YOU PLAY ON THROUGH
    THE PAIN YOU KNOW
THE RHYTHM WILL
    SUSTAIN YOU MAKE
    YOU WHOLE
SO LET YOUR FINGERS — OOH
    BLEED
YOU KNOW THAT'S JUST
    WHAT YOU NEED
YOU FEED YOUR SOUL — SOUL
YOU SAVE YOUR SOUL — OH

JUST PUT YOUR HEART

        PUT YOUR HEART…
JUST PUT YOUR HEART — PUT YOUR HEART INTO
        PUT YOUR HEART…
JUST PUT YOUR HEART — PUT YOUR HEART IN…
    INTO YOUR HANDS — AHH AHH
    AND PLAY

        PLAY

YOU HOPE AND PRAY — AHH
FOR ONE MORE DAY — AHH
THEN PUT YOUR HEART — YOUR HEART INTO YOUR
    INTO YOUR HANDS — HANDS AND
    AND PLAY

        AND PLAY…
YOU PUT YOUR HEART
    INTO YOUR HANDS
    AND PLAY

MOUNA. Oh hello. You're back? What did the lawyer say?

WALTER. The petition for asylum is before the court.

MOUNA. So, we wait.

WALTER. I'm sure they'll rule for Tarek.

MOUNA. I'm not so sure.

WALTER. Mrs. Khalil... Mouna.

MOUNA. Please. Keep practicing.

(He stands, but she waves him off.)

WALTER. Well – all right. I sound a lot better when he's playing with me.

MOUNA. Don't worry, Tarek didn't sound that great at the beginning either.

*(The phone rings. **MOUNA** is passing so she answers it. We hear **CHARLES**' voice.)*

Maybe it's the lawyer. Hello? ...

CHARLES. *(On phone.)* Ah, I'm sorry, I think I may have dialed the wrong number, I was looking for Walter...

MOUNA. No, you've dialed the correct number. Who is this?

CHARLES. *(On phone.)* Charles Van Horne.

MOUNA. *(Looks to **WALTER**.)* Charles Van Horne?

*(**WALTER** shakes his head indicating he does not want to speak with **CHARLES**.)*

I'm sorry, he's not in at present. May I take a message?

CHARLES. *(On phone.)* Um yes. Could you ask him to call me immediately? I've left five messages and emailed.

MOUNA. Of course.

CHARLES. *(On phone.)* ...The dean is asking questions – He needs to show his face. This week.

MOUNA. I'll be sure to pass this on. Does he have your number?

CHARLES. *(On phone.)* Absolutely. Can I ask who this is?

MOUNA. A family friend. Thank you, Charles.

> *(She puts down the phone and looks to* **WALTER**, *who looks a little like a naughty schoolboy.)*

How did you say your teaching was going?

WALTER. Fine. Well… I have a lighter schedule so I can focus on my book.

MOUNA. Your book? What is it about?

WALTER. Well, it covers quite a bit, so it's hard to explain.

MOUNA. You don't like to talk about your work?

WALTER. No, it's just not a process that's easy to talk about with someone who's not a writer.

MOUNA. Oh.

WALTER. I shouldn't have spoken to you like that.

MOUNA. It's okay.

WALTER. I'm – I'm very frustrated. By everything.

MOUNA. I am too. You should go back to work.

WALTER. I want to be here.

MOUNA. Why?

> *(Beat as he searches.)*

Who else is able to visit Tarek?

> *(Beat.* **WALTER** *stares at* **MOUNA** *– "Let me do this." She hears him and smiles.)*

Okay.

WALTER. I'm going to make some food.

MOUNA. But I've prepared what I was going to make in my mind already.

WALTER. So have I! I'd enjoy cooking for someone other than myself.

MOUNA. Okay. You can cook tomorrow!

[MUSIC NO. 16A – THE FLEA MARKET]

(Lights.)

(Flea Market.)

*(**ZAINAB** is at her stall. **ZINZI**, a fellow stall holder, walks past **ZAINAB**.)*

ZINZI. Ça va, Zainab?

ZAINAB. Qui, ça va. And how did we do today?

*(**ZINZI** takes a dress off the rail.)*

ZINZI. It was rubbish. These tourists aren't paying enough for my work. But I did get something new in.

(Teasing.) I think it's a bit young for you.

ZAINAB. Young? What the hell you saying?

(They both burst out laughing.)

ZINZI. It's good to see you smile though girl. You holding up okay?

ZAINAB. I'm holding.

*(**ZAINAB** gently touches her arm as if to say thanks for asking. She sees **WALTER** approaching.)*

ZINZI. I'm praying for you every day.

ZAINAB. Oh, excuse me a moment huh.

(**ZINZI** *leaves, looking back at* **WALTER** *as he arrives.*)

What happened?

WALTER. *(Calming.)* Nothing.

ZAINAB. Has he been fighting?

WALTER. I don't think so.

ZAINAB. You don't think so?

WALTER. Zainab, I'm just saying if he has, then he has not told me.

(*Beat.*)

ZAINAB. Would you tell me if he had?

(**WALTER** *does not reply.* **ZAINAB** *looks around at some of the other stall holders as they try to work out what's happening. She suddenly gets very self-conscious.*)

Well, if it is not bad news, why are you here?

WALTER. I just thought it would be nice to tell you in person that the lawyer says that Tarek stands a very good chance of...

ZAINAB. They are paid to say that!

(*Her tone changes a tad.*)

Why are you at my place of work, Walter? Why are you even doing all of this?

(*He has no response.*)

My imam says, "Do charity silently or else the charity is you." Are you the charity, Walter? Because I am not...

WALTER. I'm sorry, I shouldn't have come.

(*He turns to leave. Before he does:*)

ZAINAB. When are you seeing him again?

WALTER. Tomorrow.

ZAINAB. Tell him that I have sold ALL but one of my onyx necklaces. He did not like my designs but I told him they would sell...

> (**WALTER** *laughs*.)

Also, tell him that my crazy cousin has been released from jail. If he can get out, there's hope for everyone! And tell him that I'm praying and fasting for his release and he knows how powerful my prayers are. Tell him those things for me, the rest he knows.

> (**WALTER** *leaves*.)

[MUSIC NO. 17 – BLESSINGS (AT TIMES LIKE THESE)]

ZAINAB.
> AT TIMES LIKE THESE, AT TIMES LIKE THESE
> WHEN THE WORLD IS DARK AND DAYS WEIGH ON YOUR
>   MIND
> A GIRL NEEDS ALL THE BLESSINGS SHE CAN FIND...
>
> NOW REMEMBER, FRIEND, THAT WHEN I'M GONE
> MY BLESSING STAYS WITH YOU

ZINZI.
> WHEN THE NIGHTS GET LONG,
> WHEN DAYS DRAG ON
> A BLESSING GETS YOU THROUGH

VENDOR.
> WHEN THE MORNING LULL CAN LAST ALL DAY
> A BLESSING ON EACH STALL

ANOTHER VENDOR.
> WHEN THE TOURISTS HAGGLE, HATE TO PAY

ZAINAB, ZINZI & TWO VENDORS.

A BLESSING ON THEM ALL!

ZAINAB.　　　　　　　　　　　　　　**ZINZI & ENSEMBLE.**

OH AT TIMES LIKE THESE　　　　TIMES LIKE THESE
OH AT TIMES LIKE THESE　　　　TIMES LIKE THESE
YOU CAN THROW YOUR HANDS UP　AHH
　　HIGH AND SHRUG AND SIGH　SIGH
OR SAY,

ALL.

"GOD BLESS US SOMEHOW WE'LL GET BY…"

ZINZI.

WHEN THE DAY IS HUMID, HOT, AND GREY

ALL.

A BLESSING SHOULD YOU SWOON…

CUSTOMER.

WHEN MISTER SOFTEE DRIVES OUR WAY

ALL.

A BLESSING ON HIS TUNE!

ANOTHER CUSTOMER.

WHEN THE Q AND R RUN LATE AND SLOW

ALL.

A BLESSING ON THE BUS
AND A BLESSING WITH YOU AS YOU GO
FROM EV'RY ONE OF US!

ZAINAB & ZINZI.

OH AT TIMES LIKE THESE　　　　**ENSEMBLE.**

　　　　　　　　　　　　　　　TIMES LIKE THESE

OH AT TIMES LIKE THESE

　　　　　　　　　　　　　　　TIMES LIKE THESE

THESE BLESSINGS ARE LIKE　　　AHH
　　MAGIC YOU MIGHT SAY　　　SAY

ALL.
THE MORE YOU GIVE THE MORE WILL COME YOUR WAY
THE MORE YOU LIVE THE MORE YOU GIVE
THE MORE WILL COME YOUR WAY

ZAINAB.
AT TIMES LIKE THESE
OH, AT TIMES LIKE THESE
WHEN THE DAYS TURN HARD AND COLD AS ONYX STONE
A BLESSING KNOWING YOU ARE NOT ALONE

(Walter's apartment.)

*(***MOUNA*** *presses the play button on Walter's CD player.)*

[MUSIC NO. 18 – SUCH BEAUTIFUL MUSIC]

MOUNA.
MMM...
AHH...
SUCH BEAUTIFUL MUSIC...

*(***WALTER*** *enters. She does not hear him but turns and sees him and gives a start.)*

Oh! Walter. I didn't hear you come in.

WALTER. I didn't mean to startle you.

MOUNA. I hope you don't mind...

WALTER. Of course not.

MOUNA.
SUCH A BEAUTIFUL SOUND,
SUCH A MAGICAL EASE,
THIS FLOATING MELODY...
LIKE A RAY OF THE SUN,
A SUMMERTIME BREEZE,

SO AIRY AND SO FREE…
WEAVES AN ELABORATE SPELL,
BUT SIMPLE AND FINE –
THE MUSIC OF A LIFE.
I HAVE BEEN WONDERING – WELL –
THIS MUST BE YOUR WIFE –
YES, WALTER?

WALTER. Yes.

MOUNA. She must have had a beautiful soul.

WALTER. She did.

MOUNA.	**WALTER.**
OH, SUCH A BEAUTIFUL SOUND,	SHE HAD A WAY.
SO SHINING AND CLEAR,	A GIFT.
THIS SOARING, TUNEFUL CRY.	FOR A WHILE…
HOW SUCH A GLORIOUS STRAND	A WAY WITH A TUNE,
COULD LEAVE US IN TEARS	A ROOM,
ALONE AND WOND'RING WHY?	A SMILE…
WHY SUCH A BEAUTIFUL SONG,	SHE'D PLAY…
SO BRIMMING WITH JOY,	SHE'D STOP…
COULD BE THE SOUND OF LOSS.	SHE'D WAIT…
HOW SUCH A LYRICAL LOVE,	I WOULD LISTEN,
FALLS ACROSS OUR HEARTS…	BUT TOO LATE… TOO LATE.
OUR TWO BROKEN HEARTS…	
OUR SHINING, BREAKING, BROKEN HEARTS.	OUR BROKEN HEARTS.

(This hangs a moment, then:)

WALTER. Mouna...?

MOUNA. Yes?

WALTER. I was wondering if... do you have plans Thursday night?

MOUNA. No, Walter, I have no plans.

WALTER. I was thinking, maybe we could...do something?

MOUNA. Okay.

WALTER. Okay.

(He heads into the next room. **MOUNA** *continues singing to herself.)*

MOUNA.
SUCH A BEAUTIFUL SOUND,
SUCH A MAGICAL EASE,
THIS FLOATING MELODY...
LIKE A RAY OF THE SUN,
A SUMMERTIME BREEZE,
SO AIRY AND SO FREE...

(Lights. **WALTER** *is at the Detention Center.)*

TAREK. Walter, I knew this was going to happen.

WALTER. It's alright, we have a way to...

TAREK. It's not going to work, Walter. They denied the appeal.

WALTER. Don't say that...

TAREK. *(Flash of temper.)* What do you want me to say? They said it's over.

WALTER. *(Not yielding.)* And I'm saying this is not!

TAREK. Walter, I need you to take down a letter. To Zainab.

WALTER. All right.

TAREK. First, I need you to promise me that whatever I say, whatever I tell her, you will deliver the letter – no matter what.

WALTER. Of course.

TAREK. No – I need you to swear to me.

WALTER. I swear.

TAREK. Okay.

> *(Split scene:)*

> (**ZAINAB**, *at a workbench, reading.)*

TAREK & ZAINAB. Habibti,

[MUSIC NO. 19 – MY LOVE IS FREE]

TAREK. You must do what I say, though I know you won't want to.

ZAINAB. *(Reading.)* And usually you give the orders and I follow –

> *(Smiles, despite herself.)*

– but this time you must listen.

TAREK. The city is not safe for you anymore. You need to go missing. You need to start a new life.

You may never see me again on this earth. But no force can keep us apart forever.

> (**ZAINAB** *stops reading, composes herself.)*

MY HANDS ARE AT A METAL DOOR
MY FEET ARE CUFFED IN STEEL
MY HEART – MY HEART IS HELD NO MORE
MY LOVE WILL NEVER KNEEL.

TAREK.
> AND THOUGH I'M LOCKED INSIDE THESE WALLS
> AND I MAY ALWAYS BE
> MY LOVE IS FREE
> MY LOVE IS FREE

TAREK & ZAINAB.
> MY LOVE CAN CROSS THE ALTAI STEPPE
> OR CLIMB THE ATLAS RANGE
> NO BORDER IS TOO BOLDLY DRAWN
> NO FOREIGN LAND TOO STRANGE
>
> MY LOVE IS IN THE SINAI
> AND ON THE SEVENTH SEA
> MY LOVE IS FREE
> MY LOVE IS FREE
>
> MY LOVE IS MULTITUDES, AND JUST WE TWO
> MY LOVE IS INFINITE, AND ONLY YOU
> MY LOVE IS EV'RYWHERE, A STRANGER IN STRANGE
>   LANDS
> MAY MY BODY FALL – MY LOVE STILL STANDS.

TAREK.
> MY LOVE – IT'S TIME TO SAY GOODBYE
> IT'S TIME YOU MUST MOVE ON
> IT ISN'T SAFE TO WRITE TO ME –
> IMAGINE THAT I'M GONE –

TAREK.	**ZAINAB.**

THE BEST THING YOU
    CAN DO NOW
IS PROMISE THAT TO ME –
THAT YOU'LL BE FREE –
	I'LL FIND A WAY TO DO IT –
	I PROMISE LOVE, YOU'LL
	    SEE –
	BUT LOVE IS FREE –

DETAINEES (FULL ENSEMBLE).
> LOVE IS FREE...

TAREK, ZAINAB & DETAINEES.
> OUR LOVE IS FREE –

(In shadow, we begin to see **OTHER DETAINEES** *in their cells, and other* **LOVED ONES** *waiting elsewhere for them.)*

MY LOVE IS INFINITE, MY LOVE WON'T DIE.
MY LOVE WILL LIFT YOU UP AND HOLD YOU HIGH.
MY LOVE IS EV'RYWHERE, IN LANDS BOTH NEAR AND FAR –
MY LOVE'S THE WHOLE WORLD OVER –
IT RUNS THE WHOLE WORLD OVER –
IT FLIES THE WHOLE WORLD OVER –
MY LOVE IS WHERE YOU ARE.

(Break.)

(Eventually the **GUARD** *takes* **TAREK**, *leaving* **ZAINAB** *alone.)*

(The **OTHER DETAINEES** *leave their* **LOVED ONES**, *who watch them go, then fade.)*

ZAINAB.
MY LOVE IS ON A
   CROSSTOWN STREET
OR ON AN UPTOWN TRAIN

ENSEMBLE.
ON AN UPTOWN TRAIN...

TAREK.
IT CAN'T BE BOUND BY
   HOBBLED FEET
OR HELD BY ANY CHAIN

OR HELD BY ANY CHAIN

ZAINAB & TAREK.
MY LOVE IS ANY WAY TO
   RUN

MY LOVE...

MY LOVE IS EV'RY KEY
MY LOVE IS FREE

MY LOVE IS EV'RY KEY

MY LOVE IS FREE...

MY HEART IS FREE

MY HEART IS FREE

<table>
<tr><td>ZAINAB & TAREK.</td><td>ENSEMBLE. (Variously.)</td></tr>
<tr><td>MY MIND IS FREE</td><td>MIND IS…FREE…</td></tr>
<tr><td>MY HOPE IS FREE</td><td>HOPE IS…FREE…</td></tr>
<tr><td>MY LOVE IS FREE</td><td>LOVE IS FREE</td></tr>
</table>

(Transition to:)

(Central Park.)

(WALTER *and* **MOUNA** *move through amid heated debate…)*

WALTER. …I'm so sorry, I'm not sure a walk was a good idea.

MOUNA. Don't apologize. It's a good idea. I love this park… and I needed a distraction. Walter, is that a theater?

WALTER. I think so.

MOUNA. There was this huge outdoor amphitheater in Syria before the war. We used to take Tarek to see concerts.

WALTER. Did he enjoy it?

MOUNA. Oh yes. We all did. Do you ever take your students to the theater?

WALTER. I teach economics.

MOUNA. All the more reason.

WALTER. Actually, I'm thinking of taking a leave of absence for the rest of the semester.

MOUNA. What about your work, Walter?

WALTER. Truth is, I haven't done any real work in a long time. I've been teaching the same course for twenty years and it doesn't mean anything to me. None of it does.

(A moment. Her heart opens as she sees this is about her son.)

MOUNA. Walter, what would you do if you didn't teach?

WALTER. I don't know.

MOUNA. Please don't do this for us.

WALTER. I'm not.

(*Beat.*)

MOUNA. Then I think that's… Good.

(*Beat.*)

(**WALTER***'s phone buzzes. He checks it.*)

WALTER. That's the lawyer. Damn it!

MOUNA. What is it?

WALTER. They're moving him to another facility.

MOUNA. What facility? Where?

WALTER. She doesn't know.

[MUSIC NO. 19A – THE DETENTION CENTER 2]

(*Transition to:*)

(*Detention Center.*)

(*A* **GUARD** *at a desk.*)

(**WALTER** *hurries in.*)

Excuse me. I'm here for bed thirty-eight. Tarek Khalil.

GUARD. Visiting hours end at ten p.m.

WALTER. I understand, but this is extremely urgent. Could you please check for me?

(*The* **GUARD** *taps at a computer.*)

GUARD. He's no longer with us.

WALTER. What does that mean?

GUARD. He's been removed.

WALTER. Removed? To where?

GUARD. He's been deported.

WALTER. Deported? When?

GUARD. This afternoon.

WALTER. He – how can that be? Is there any way to contact him?

GUARD. I don't think so.

WALTER. You don't think so? What kind of answer is that?

GUARD. I'm sorry, sir. That's all the information that I have. Now please step away from the desk. You can contact ICE if you have any further questions. Here's the number.

 (**WALTER** *does not move.*)

Sir. Please step away from my desk.

 (*Then.*)

Sir. For the last time, step away from my desk.

 (**WALTER** *turns to go and turns back.*)

[MUSIC NO. 20 – BETTER ANGELS]

WALTER. You can't just take people away like that. It's not fair. This man... This man...

THIS MAN, HE WAS A GOOD MAN, WITH A LIFE AND YEARS
 TO LIVE
THIS MAN DESERVED THE BEST OF WHAT THIS COUNTRY
 HAS TO GIVE
AND NO JUST LAW WOULD MEAN THAT SUCH A MAN
 SHOULD DISAPPEAR,
WE'RE NOT JUST HELPLESS CHILDREN –

DO YOU HEAR ME? DO YOU HEAR?
DO YOU HEAR?

WE HAVE BETRAYED OUR BETTER ANGELS
THE ONES THAT ONCE SHOWED US THE WAY
THE BETTER ANGELS OF OUR NATURE –
ARE THEY LOST TO US TODAY?

GUARD. Sir.

WALTER.
WELL, IT ISN'T YOURS TO SAY.

THIS MAN WHO THEY HAVE VANISHED,
LIKE A MURDER, LIKE A GHOST –
THIS MAN IS AN AMERICAN,
IN ALL THAT MATTERS MOST.
BOTH TIRELESS AND FEARLESS,
FULL OF MUSIC, PROUD AND FREE...
IF SUCH A MAN CAN DISAPPEAR,
THEN WHY NOT YOU AND ME?
WHY NOT ME?

WHEN DID WE LOSE OUR BETTER ANGELS?
HOW DID WE LEAVE THEM IN OUR WAKE?
HOW DID WE SACRIFICE OUR TRUEST CAUSE
FOR SOME SMALL COMFORT'S SAKE?

WE KNOW COMPASSION IS NOT WEAKNESS,
AND THAT TRUE JUSTICE IS NOT BLIND.
BUT WE HAVE LOST OUR BETTER ANGELS –
WE HAVE LEFT THEM FAR BEHIND.

IT'S SUCH A POOR PATHETIC SIGHT:
ONE OLD WHITE MAN, ONE ERRANT KNIGHT,
AWAKENED TO THIS WORLD AT LAST.

BUT IF THERE IS A GOD, WELL, THEN,
A THOUSAND OLD AND TIRED WHITE MEN,
A MILLION OLD AND SCARED WHITE MEN,
WILL WAKE UP JUST LIKE ME –

WALTER.

AND FAST...
AND FAST...

AND WE MUST FIND OUR BETTER ANGELS,
AND OUR COUNTRY'S STOLEN SOUL.
AND REMEMBER WHERE WE CAME FROM.
AND MAKE WHAT'S BROKEN WHOLE.

FOR WE WERE BORN IN REVOLUTION
AND WE WERE BUILT ON RIGHTS OF MEN
WHEN WE FIGHT, WE SAY FOR FREEDOM
WILL WE KNOW FREEDOM ONCE AGAIN?

FOR WE WARRIORS OF FREEDOM,
WE HAVE UP AND WE'VE DESERTED...
AM I PREACHING TO THE CHOIR?
WELL, THE CHOIR'S NOT CONVERTED.

THEY SAY A SINGLE VOICE CANNOT BE HEARD ABOVE
THE ROAR
SO WE'LL RAISE A MILLION VOICES AND AS ONE WE'LL
SAY – NO MORE.

AND SEEK OUR BETTER ANGELS
WE WILL FIND OUR BETTER ANGELS
WE WILL KNOW OUR BETTER ANGELS
WE PRAY
WE WILL EMBRACE OUR BETTER ANGELS ONE DAY!

[MUSIC NO. 21 – MY LOVE IS FREE (REPRISE)]

ZAINAB.

MY LOVE IS MULTITUDES, AND JUST WE TWO
MY LOVE IS INFINITE, AND ONLY YOU
MY LOVE IS EV'RYWHERE, IT CROSSES EV'RY SEA
AS FAR AS YOU MAY GO
YOU'RE HERE WITH ME...

(Lights.)

(Transition to:)

(Walter's apartment.)

[MUSIC NO. 22 – WHAT LITTLE I CAN DO]

*(Early evening. **WALTER** at the window, staring out. **MOUNA** enters with suitcases.)*

WALTER. Mouna...?

MOUNA. I need to be where Tarek is.

WALTER. How will you get there?

MOUNA. It doesn't matter.

WALTER. Do you even know where he is?

MOUNA. I'll find him!

WALTER. Mouna this doesn't make sense.

MOUNA. *(Firmly.)* Walter, it's my fault – What happened to Tarek. We *did* receive the letter telling us to leave and I threw it away. I had found a job. Tarek was in school... everyone told me not to worry. That the government didn't care. For a time that seemed true. And then after a time, you forget. You think that you really belong.

It's best for me to leave now.

WALTER. Mouna.

MOUNA.
HE NEEDS MY HAND, HE NEEDS MY CARE
MY PRECIOUS BOY WHO DID NO WRONG
I DON'T KNOW WHAT AWAITS HIM THERE
IT'S CHANGED SO MUCH, AND WE'VE BEEN HERE SO LONG

WALTER.
WE'LL ASK THE COURT FOR AN APPEAL –
THE CONFLICT OVER THERE IS REAL

MOUNA.

DEAR WALTER, NO, THAT TIME IS THROUGH
I MUST BE THERE TO DO
WHAT LITTLE I CAN DO

WALTER.

IT'S NOT YOUR FAULT, I HOPE THAT'S CLEAR.
YOU CHASED A DREAM TO THIS NEW SHORE...
A LIFE OF HOPE, AND FREE FROM FEAR...
YOU'RE EV'RYTHING THIS COUNTRY SHOULD STAND FOR.

MOUNA.

THIS LAND THEY SAY IS FOR THE FREE
NO LONGER FEELS THAT WAY TO ME
IT'S NOT THE LAND OF HOPE I KNEW
AND 'TIL NOW I NEVER KNEW
WHAT LITTLE I CAN DO
WE GIVE OUR CHILDREN ALL WE CAN

WALTER & MOUNA.

WE MAKE THE LIFE THAT WE CAN MAKE

WALTER.

YOUR BOY'S A GOOD AND GIVING MAN
THE TALE YOU TOLD, YOU TOLD FOR TAREK'S SAKE

MOUNA.

THIS WORLD IS DARK, BOTH NIGHT AND DAY
NO WISH CAN WASH THE HURT AWAY

WALTER.

NO HURT IS EASY TO SUBDUE
BUT STILL, SOMEHOW, WE DO
WHAT LITTLE WE CAN DO

WALTER & MOUNA.

STILL, SOMEHOW, WE DO
WHAT LITTLE WE CAN DO

[MUSIC NO. 22A – SUCH BEAUTIFUL MUSIC (REPRISE)]

(**MOUNA** *hands* **WALTER** *a small pouch.*)

MOUNA. Here. Zainab asked me to give this to you.

(*He opens it. A bracelet from Zainab's table.*)

WALTER. Thank you. It's very nice.

MOUNA. Let me see.

(*She puts it on his wrist.*)

WALTER. I like it.

MOUNA. So do I... Thank you, Walter. For everything.

WALTER. I didn't do anything...at all. I don't want you to go.

MOUNA. I know, habibi.

(*She leaves, closing the door behind her.* **WALTER** *sits in his chair.*)

[MUSIC NO. 23 – DRUM CIRCLE (REPRISE)]

(**WALTER** *stands, bereft, as the apartment disappears around him.*)

(**MOUNA** *walks out of the door and onto the street.*)

(*The wall moves to reveal* **MOUNA**.)

ENSEMBLE. (*A cappella.*)
HERE I AM... (HERE I AM...)

(**TAREK** *enters.*)

HERE I AM... (HERE I AM...)

(**ZAINAB** *enters.*)

ENSEMBLE.
HERE I AM...
HERE I AM...

WALTER.
RHYTHM IS NEVER A THING THAT YOU FIND OUTSIDE YOU
RHYTHM IS NOT LIKE A TRAIN THAT YOU CHASE IN VAIN

TAREK.
RHYTHM IS LIFE AND DEATH, THE TURNING TIDES,
    THE BREATH OF RAIN

MOUNA.
RHYTHM WILL HOLD YOU, LIFT YOU, TAKE YOU,
    GUIDE YOU
RHYTHM WILL SHOW YOU THE WAY THAT YOU FIND
    YOUR WAY

TAREK.
DON'T WORRY ON LEARNING A PART
JUST LISTEN HARD TO YOUR HEART AND PLAY

ZAINAB.	**ENSEMBLE.**
LISTEN TO ALL AROUND YOU AND YOU'LL HEAR IT	OH
LISTEN WITH LOVE, AND LEARN BEFORE YOU'RE DONE	OH

MOUNA & WALTER.	
THE CIRCLE ENCIRCLES US ALL	OH
	THE CIRCLE ENCIRCLES US ALL
WE STAND OR ELSE WE FALL AS ONE...	WE FALL AS

ZAINAB.
FALL AS ONE...

TAREK.
FALL AS

ALL.

ONE

(Eventually the **DRUM CIRCLE** *forms around him joining in until it becomes a defiant, urgent, rising finale.)*

THAT'S HOW WE JOIN THE CIRCLE
THAT'S HOW WE MAKE OF MANY SONGS ONE SONG
THAT'S HOW WE JOIN THE CIRCLE

THAT'S HOW WE'RE STRONG
STRONGER IN THE CIRCLE
WHERE WE HEAR THE BEAT OF MANY HEARTS

TAREK, WALTER, ZAINAB & MOUNA.	**ENSEMBLE GROUP 1**.	**ENSEMBLE GROUP 2**.
BEATING IN THE CIRCLE	WE SING ALONG	HERE I AM
SINGING IN THE CIRCLE	WE SING ALONG	HERE I AM
SO WE JOIN		

ALL.

THE CIRCLE
LIVE INSIDE THE CIRCLE
STEP INTO THE CIRCLE

TAREK.

AND SOMETHING STARTS

ENSEMBLE.

OH OH OH
OH OH OH
OH OH OH
OH OH OH
OH OH OH

*(***WALTER** *and* **TAREK** *begin to play. As* **TAREK** *plays with increasing force, he fades out.)*

ENSEMBLE.
OH OH OH
OH OH OH
OH OH OH
OH OH OH

(**WALTER** *drums alone with increasing intensity until he crashes down on the drum, bringing us to:)*

The End